Cover Design: Jai Ellis
Editing: Rachel Benson
https://www.facebook.com/Pleasemeseries
http://www.twitter.com/iamobsession
http://obsessionthewriter.tumblr.com
https://www.facebook.com/I.AM.OBSESSI
ON
https://www.facebook.com/Obsessionthewrit
er

Table of contents

Dear reader

Introduction

Dear reader,

This note is being written to you out of gratitude and love. I'll forever be grateful to you for taking a chance and stepping into my creative world. Many writers write for many reasons, I myself write to form a bond with the world. The stories I write aren't completely fiction, you will find bits and pieces of my life within them all. If you're afraid to 'feel' my books aren't for you. Every emotion I've ever felt in my life is poured into my stories; from pain all the way to sexual exploitations. I want to connect with other people who can relate to the things I've been through, and the things my characters go through; sometimes that's all it takes is to know that you're not alone in this world. Well friends, I hope you enjoy the story! Oh and please don't forget to leave a review!

Hugs~Love~& Smiles,
~OBSESSION~

PLEASURE PALACE
~An erotic romance~

PROLOGUE

He had decided the night before that he was going to go through with his plan. From the moment they announced their engagement, he knew that he had to come up with something to end their relationship, a relationship that shouldn't have happened in the first place. It angered him every time he saw them hugging or kissing or even being near each other. It pissed him off every time Jeremy would talk about Kara to him, because it felt like he was rubbing their happiness in his face. He was so sick of getting fitted for the wedding, going to rehearsals, and acting interested in helping plan the bachelor's party. He couldn't care less about that got damn wedding, and he was tired of suppressing his feelings of disgust for the both of them.

He used to like her a lot... a hell of a lot, until she played him like a video game and chose Jeremy instead. Honestly, he'd find himself gazing and fantasizing about her; lusting and craving to be the one between her legs every single night. He first saw Kara at a bowling alley called Ten Pins next to The House of Blues located downtown. She stood out from the other two ladies she was with, so much that he couldn't take his eyes off of her. He'd finally worked up the nerves to talk to her, so he caught her at the bar getting a pitcher of water refilled. He politely introduced himself and asked her name. She flashed that radiant smile of hers and shook his outstretched hand. He asked her for her number and that's when she hit him with some straight bullshit.

"Oh I'm sorry, but you're not the type I usually go for. I have my eyes on your friend over there."

He guessed the look on his face said it all, because Kara apologized two more times before heading back to her lane. He called himself being a good sport by letting his friend know that he was trying to holler at her, but she wanted Jeremy instead. He seriously thought that with Jeremy being his best friend, he wouldn't try to go after her. Wrong! Jeremy did the complete opposite and that pissed him off even more. He managed to fake the funk for the rest of the night and had fun with his boys. He just kept telling himself that she'd be a hit it and quit it... nothing more or nothing less. Once again he was wrong. Three years later Jeremy and Kara were getting married.

That was the straw that broke the camel's back. He was furious and couldn't hold it in anymore. Something had to be done. He pulled into the parking lot of his destination and sat inside of the car going over everything in his head. He'd driven for damn near an hour to get up there, so he might as well go through with it.

"Welcome back sir. You're becoming a real regular here! Eden is expecting you, so you can go right up that spiral staircase to her office."

"Thank you Cory." He replied.

A wave of guilt swept over him as he climbed the stairs to Eden's office. Shame hit him in the chest in mid-step, but he quickly pushed it out of his mind and found the woman he was looking for. He heard a lamp crash to the floor and a high pitched cry that escalated into loud invigorating moans.

"Eden, should I come back later? You seem a little busy."

That nut must have been good, because the man inside said every curse word known to man before collapsing to the floor. When Eden opened the door two things could be seen: her naked body and a man lying on the floor glistening like he'd just stepped out of the shower.

"Hey there baby boy, you got here quicker than I expected. Come on in."

The stench of sex drop-kicked him right in the nose, and she could tell by the look on his face that his stomach was doing flips.

"Oh please! Don't act like you haven't smelled dick and pussy before. How in the hell do you think it smells after we get done fucking each other, silly? Go on, take a good sniff. The smell of sex is so freaking exciting, isn't it? Just makes you want to juice all day long! Have a seat and tell me what's up."

He stepped over the sweaty man who was still huffing and puffing like he'd just ran a marathon and took a seat across from her.

Page 8

"I need a huge favor. Actually it's a gigantic favor. I need for you, my love, to help me carry out this plan I've cooked up." he said.

"And what plan would that be?" she asked while pouring Grey Goose into a couple of glasses.

"I need you to help me break up my best friend and his fiancée. They are scheduled to get married one week from this Saturday, and I need it to be called off." he replied.

Eden slid his glass across the desk and then took a deep swig of vodka from her own.

"Why? Why do you want to do this, and how can I be of some assistance?" she questioned.

He took his entire glass of liquor to the head before responding. He pushed the glass towards her and leaned back in his chair.

"We have a mutual friend that I overheard talking on the phone about coming to this club. We're all supposed to hang out this Saturday and I'm guessing that she's going to suggest coming here. If we end up here, I need Cory, Shawn, you and everyone that works here to act like they don't know me. My friends do not know that I'm a regular here. I need you to switch some things around and alter the rules a bit to make sure that we're all in separate rooms. I want my best friend and his girl to get so worked out that they'll be unsure whether or not they should get married... well at least so soon. I want you to put your best male and female pleasers on them for the entire night. Can you make that happen for me?"

She walked around her desk and handed him another glass of vodka.

"Sure I can do that. What are their names?"

"Jeremy and Kara."

"Jeremy and Kara... cute, but you still haven't told me why you want to destroy their relationship?"

"You really want to know why?"

He slammed the glass onto the desk and walked towards the door.
"Because if I can't have what I want, then no one can."

PART I: THE CHALLENGE

<u>CHAPTER I</u>

Kara looked over at her soon-to-be husband and placed her hand over her heart. She had dreamed of getting married to her Prince Charming since she was a little girl, and a week from today she'd be doing just that. They had been together for three wonderful years and she couldn't be happier. Of course they had their ups and downs like any other normal couple, but love just always prevailed. She often pinched herself to see if she was dreaming. Jeremy was flawless. He's tall, dark and handsome with confidence that could easily be mistaken for arrogance. His bank account could end hunger around the world and in the bedroom... well he's an outright beast! That last fact made Kara throb down below and her sudden shiver caught her fiancé's attention.

"Thinking about me baby?" Jeremy asked.

Kara bit her bottom lip and slowly nodded yes.

"Wait until our wedding night. You haven't had the best of me yet. Baby the things I'm going to do to you..."

He licked his lips and signaled for her to sit on his lap.

"No can do honey. You know what happens whenever our lower halves touch. Shit gets X-rated real quick and that wouldn't be a good idea since we're expecting company."

Just as Jeremy was about to object the doorbell rang.

"I'll get it. I don't want them to see that big wet spot between your legs." He teased.

Kara snatched a decorative pillow from the couch and popped him in the back of the head with it.

"Baby come on now, you haven't won a pillow fight against me yet, so stop it. You don't want any of those problems." he warned.

"Whatever. Just open the door already. I bet Bren and Xavier have tried to strangle each other the few seconds they've been waiting outside of the door. Those two work my nerves to no end!"

Jeremy shook his head and laughed.

"I wish they would just have sex and get it over with, seriously. I mean, they know that they want to. They probably masturbate at night while thinking about one another."

As soon as he cracked the door he could hear his two friends bickering with each other.

"Want you? Boy nobody wants your LL Cool J wanna-be ass, so have a seat! Ooh wee! This dude doesn't stop!"

"Bren you are too damn grown not to admit when you want some dick. If you want me to bang your brains out just say so. We can do it right here and right now, because Lord knows you need a good hard nut to put your ass to sleep."

Jeremy looked over at the other two guests that were dying of laughter from the Bren and Xavier show.

"Hey Aleric and Chassidy. How long have these two fools been going at it?"

"As soon as they stepped out of their cars they were at each other's necks. Xavier started it though." said Aleric.

"As usual." Chassidy added.

"Xavier, what makes you think that I need to be put to sleep? For your information, I'm the one who puts folks to bed, thank you very much!" said Bren.

"Because I know your ass is tired from running your mouth all damn day. I mean you never shut up. I have something for that though. Open your mouth." he retorted.

"Forget you Xavier. Anyway, how is my best friend doing? Only one week until the big day! Are you excited?"

Bren plopped down on the sofa next to her friend still awaiting her answer.

"Bren I'm ecstatic! After three years I'll finally be Mrs. Jeremy James. I couldn't be happier." Kara stated.

"Yea, yea, yea, enough of that mushy shit, we get it. Y'all are in love and are getting married... over it! Have we decided on what we're going to do tonight?" Xavier asked impatiently.

"I'm starving! Let's go have dinner at that Creole joint on The Magnificent Mile called Heaven on Seven. Their barbecue salmon is to die for." Chassidy suggested.

"Hell no! That place is always packed on Saturday nights, and I refuse to wait almost an hour for a table. Sorry but no can do." said Kara.

"I second that, Kara. We'd be packed in that place like people at a Janet Jackson concert."

"How about bowling? We've been talking about doing that for a few months now." said Aleric.

"*Y'all* have been talking about going bowling. You know I don't stick my feet in anyone else's shoes. I don't give a damn if they spray them down or not. I can't do it. Let's just go out and get some drinks. After my work week, I need to toss back a few." said Xavier.

"There's this club called the Pleasure Palace over on North and Clybourn. Let's go there." Bren said while looking into her pocket mirror.

PLEASURE PALACE

"I'm so sick of you and that gotdamn mirror. Nothing has changed. You're still ugly as hell." said Xavier.

"Xay, behave please." Kara insisted.

"The Pleasure Palace? I think I overheard some guys at the gym talking about that place. It's that new sex club that opened a few months back in the spring right? Jeremy asked.

"Yep, I heard it was off the chain, and the people in there be doing all types of freaky shit you didn't even know was possible or even existed." said Bren.

"Oh my! Go on...tell me more." Chassidy insisted.

"Okay I was at the nail salon getting a pedicure when this chick sits in the chair next me talking loud on her cellphone. I was about to ask her to shut the hell up but then she said to whomever she was talking to that one dude was feeding her exotic fruits while the other one was eating her out and how that person needed to come with her the next time she went to that club. So my nosy ass asked her what club was she referring to and to tell me more about it. Chile she was telling me some off the wall stuff about how in one room they were having an orgy, in another room women were switching off giving several men head, and in other rooms there was lesbian sex, gay sex… She said even senior citizens were in there bumping uglies!" said Bren.

"Shit, count me in!" shouted Xavier.

"Hell, me too. I'm definitely interested in going to check it out." said Aleric.

"That day I bumped into you guys at the auto show, I was on the phone trying to get one of my fuck buddies to come to the club with me, but he was making up excuses about why he couldn't go to a place like that. He was just scared if you ask me. Even though he's a good one, he's not the wildest, freakiest lover I've had the pleasure of dropping it like it's hot on." Bren admitted.

"I'm kind of curious about it myself. What about you, Kara?" asked Chassidy.

"Please! My baby and I already get it popping on the sex tip. We don't need to go to some sex club to get freaky, do we baby?"

PLEASURE PALACE

Kara leaned over and kissed Jeremy on the cheek.

"We sure don't baby. We'd be tearing this house up right now if y'all weren't here. I was just telling Kara before you guys came that the night of our wedding was going to be epic. I'm trying to break a record that night." said Jeremy with confidence.

Xavier made the 'your breath sinks' face at his friend's comment.

Bren put her make-up kit back inside her purse and placed her hand on Kara's shoulder.

"Oh my dear friend... It's okay to say the real reason why you don't want you and your man to go to a sex club, Kara. We all know the truth."

"Say what? Well what's the *real* reason Bren, since you seem to have all of the answers?" Kara snapped.

Bren threw her hands in the air and laughed.

"Calm down friend, all I'm saying is you brag to Chassidy and me all the time about how good Jeremy is in bed, so it's clear that you don't want anyone else getting a piece of that." She flicked her hand at Jeremy.

"And him too. He can't fathom another man licking or running up in that. I believe this entire three year relationship was built on sex and will fall because of it."

"Bren, what the hell are you saying?" Now Jeremy was getting pissed.

"What I'm saying is that if you two do choose to go to Pleasure Palace with us, you will not walk out of there the way you went in. There will be no wedding. I guarantee it." she answered.

Kara stood up in her friend's face and stared briefly before speaking.

"I don't appreciate you coming into my home making accusations that our relationship is shallow and weak. Jeremy's and my relationship runs on more than just mere sex. We've lasted this long because of trust, honesty, romance and love. Go home and pick out one of the many whorish outfits you have and meet me back here in two hours, because we're going to that club."

"Come on baby, we don't have to prove anything to her. Bren, I think you should leave." Jeremy said pointing to the front door.

"No baby I want to do this. I want to go. It is 8:30 now. Everybody meet us back here no later than 10:30." said Kara.

Jeremy turned Kara around to face him and searched her eyes with his. She was angry. He knew that whenever Kara was offended or felt challenged, there was no stopping her from proving her challenger wrong. The smirk on Bren's face told him that she knew that as well.

"Okay, if you're down then I'm down. We'll see y'all back here in a couple of hours; now let me walk y'all out." said Jeremy.

"Don't forget to shave your Christmas, Kara. You don't want men going down and coming back up with a goatee." Bren said on her way out. 'Christmas' is the nickname for vagina the girls created back in high school.

Jeremy slammed the door in Bren's face and looked at Kara.

"You know, I never really liked her. Baby we don't have to do this."

"Yes we do. I bet she's not the only one of our friends who thinks our relationship has made it this far solely on sex. We love each other, don't we?!" yelled Kara.

"Yes we do."

"I know! That's why we're going to prove that giving each other permission to have sex with complete strangers will not ruin us. Now let's get ready.

Jeremy shook his head and watched his fiancée scurry into their bedroom.

PLEASURE PALACE

<u>CHAPTER II</u>

<u>Jeremy and Kara</u>

Kara tore up their walk-in closet for thirty minutes trying to find the sexiest outfit and stilettos that she owned. She finally came up for air with a lemon steel-boned corset with black lace detail, a black peek-a-boo skirt with a pair of yellow and black laced ankle boots. She laid her outfit and heels across the bed and headed into the bathroom for a quick shower and run over with a razor. Even though she was pretty good with keeping her vagina and other places shaved, Bren's smart-mouthed comment made her self-conscious so she had to make sure that she was nice and lined up down there.

Jeremy watched Kara get prepared to let another man enter her sanctuary with a tad bit of irritation. Hers was a sanctuary he thought he'd be the last man to ever enter. Kara was 5'3 with dark brown skin and eyes. She had a small waist with the perfect sized breasts and a firm, plump ass. On top of that, she had a high profile career as a celebrity chef. She was beautiful with bank… a real gift.

Every part of him wanted to put an end to this juvenile challenge, but he knew that it would only cause an argument between them. He knew that Kara loved him, but wondered if she'd be pleased tonight in a way he's never been able to please her. What if she decided after tonight that marrying him was not what she wanted anymore?

"God, now you know that I love Kara with every fiber of my being, and you also know that I try not to be a violent man, but if I lose my future wife to a freak-a-leek club, I'm killing everybody! I'm starting with Bren's 'soak up nut like a sponge' ass first." Jeremy covered his mouth.

"Oops, sorry Lord, I didn't mean to curse, but as you can see, I'm a little uptight."

"Babe who are you talking to?" Kara asked while drying off in the mirror.

"Nobody. It took you long enough in there. When I come out of the bathroom, you better be ready Kara." he stated.

"Ugh, what's your problem? I'll be ready in time gosh!"

He shook his head and disappeared behind the shower curtain. Kara knew why he was so snappy, but she was too. The thought of him making love to another woman made her skin crawl. Any other time she'd probably try to set him and the chick on fire if she'd caught him creeping on her, but this time was an exception. Yes sex is a major part of their relationship, but so is communication, loyalty, honesty, fun, and most importantly, love. Bren doesn't know what the hell she's talking about, and this little challenge of hers was going to come back and bite her on the ass.

Jeremy pulled the shower curtain back and did a double-take. She was beautiful...sexy. She removed the curling iron from her hair, leaving one thick spiraled curl draping over her right eye.

PLEASURE PALACE

"Who do you think you are, Aaliyah?" He took a swat at her curls and sang the lyrics to 'One in a Million'.

"Stop playing before you mess up my hair. Come here and tighten my corset in the back. I can't reach it."

He walked up behind her and ran his fingers down her back.

"You sure are putting in a lot of effort to give another man my goodies."

She could see the concern in his eyes, so she turned to face him.

"You know I'm yours. Period. This won't change a thing between us and you know that. Jeremy, you're not the only one who's nervous and worried, but I think this will be fun and good for us. Don't you?"

"Fun? Yes I think it will be. Good for us? I'm not so sure about that. What I do know is if you walk up out that joint on another man's arm, I'm blowing the whole place up!"

Kara laughed.

"No worries baby. You just make sure one of those chicks doesn't come knocking on the door nine months later asking for child support."

"Never that baby... never that. You're my only future baby mama." he assured her.

"You never know, we might end up in a room together."

"Yea, then I'll be able to give you a taste of our honeymoon."

"No I mean we may end up in the same room with one of our friends: You with the girls and me with the guys." said Kara.

The look on Jeremy's face told her that she shouldn't have planted that possibility in his head.

"Baby I was just saying. It might not even happen, so please calm down before you prevent yourself from having a good time tonight." She placed her hand on his chest.

"Jeremy what is going through your head right now?"

"I hope I don't go to jail tonight."

Bren

PLEASURE PALACE

Bren smiled at herself for the fortieth time in the mirror. She knew that the dress she'd chosen for the evening screamed 'fuck me and fuck me good'. Black with a plunging neckline and sassy cut-outs on the sides and mid-section. Her dress was so visually distracting, that it was sure to lure in all of the freaks.

"Yes ma'am, you are ready to get banged out tonight! I hope everyone else has their own agendas for tonight, because I'm disappearing on their asses as soon as I step through the door. Wait, who am I kidding? It's not just the dress, I'm fine as hell!"

At least that was what she'd heard her entire life. Her mother had her modeling since before she could walk. She learned at a young age that beauty can get you a lot of things and take you a lot places. Being a mixed breed got her major modeling contracts with Victoria Secret, Michael Kors, and many other high fashion moguls. Boys to men have always fawned over her coffee and cream complexion, gray eyes and long wavy brown hair with natural honey blonde highlights that she inherited from her

Dutch mother. She had one large dimple in her right cheek that she borrowed from her Jamaican father. She slid into her black Anikka heels and checked herself over one last time.

"Damn Bren, you are a bad bitch!"

Chassidy

"If Bren doesn't bring her ass on, I'm leaving her."

Chassidy was sent to Bren's voicemail for the fourth time. She'd been sitting outside for over ten minutes. She was already nervous about going to a sex club, and Bren wasn't helping her nervousness by making her think that she bailed out on her. Even though people tell her that she's a beautiful woman, Chassidy has always been self-conscious. She was as dark as night with slanted hazel eyes. She had a noticeable cleft in her chin and soft laugh lines around her big plump lips. She always felt that she had odd features, but all of her male co-workers at NBC Chicago said that she should be in front of the camera instead of being the producer. She has always had thick legs so she knew that this thigh hugging gold dress she was wearing was going to draw out the thirst in the men at the club. Chassidy rolled her eyes when she saw Bren approaching her car.

"Damn girl what took you so long? We're going to be late getting to Kara and Jeremy's place."

"Chassidy, don't start with me. You know it takes time to look this good. Well… maybe you don't." she laughed.

"I'm lying! You know it doesn't take anything but for me to open my eyes every morning to look this good. I am a natural beauty baby doll. If you must know, I was on the phone with one of my banks." replied Bren.

Chassidy decided to let that smart remark about her looks go.

"One of your banks? Bren how many companies are you banking with?" Chassidy asked confused.

"Chile not those kinds of banks. I'm talking about a man. He's late paying my car note and my car insurance, so he's on punishment until he pays those plus the late fees he got me."

"So you're fucking men for bill money?" Chassidy asked incredulously.

"Yes ma'am I am. That's why I'm so fired up to go to this club tonight. I get to bust it wide open just for fun. I haven't done that in a long time."

Chassidy shook her head.

"You are just too damn much for me Bren, but I love ya."

"I love you too girl. Now let's go since you were rushing me and shit. Did you trim up your Christmas? You don't want a man to get a fur ball stuck in this throat and choke to death. I don't have any money to get your ass out of jail. I'm going to Rio de Janeiro next month and I need all of my dough, thank you!" Bren teased.

"Shut up! I keep my ole girl shaved, thank you very much! Just because I'm not out here popping my pussy like you, that does not mean I don't keep myself shaved and fresh." said Chassidy.

"Good, now maybe you can get some dick from a real man and not that vibrating plastic black thing that you keep on the side of your bed, because whew chile it looks all raggedy and lopsided… you have broken that thing all the way down like Mary J. Blige baby."

Chassidy laughed.

"Kiss my ass Bren! Why in the hell were you looking through my things anyway?"

"I wanted to find out why in the hell you didn't answer your phone after ten o'clock at night. I knew you weren't working like you lied and said you were." Bren replied.

"Now how do you know I wasn't working Bren?" Chassidy inquired.

"Because you rolled over on your phone one night and accidentally called me. Girl, I heard everything! You were working yourself out!" Bren said laughing.

Xavier

Xavier stuffed about five condoms into his pants pocket. He was ready to tear the lining out of some pussy, and he needed to make sure that he was well prepared. There wasn't much for him to do to get ready but shower and change clothes, because he always kept himself well groomed just for his everyday life. He always had to stay fresh and in shape. Being an NBA agent presented him with many groupies just like his clients. With Allen Iverson features and a fat bank account, women flocked to him like a moth to a flame.

"Oooo wee! You a sexy muthafucka Xay! You're about to set a record tonight boy! Man Aleric need to hurry the hell up. I'm ready to stroke some pretty kitties and put them down to sleep."

Aleric

Aleric wasn't as handsome as Xavier and Jeremy, so chicks didn't flock to him like they did his best friends.

Although he was average looking, he had something that only a few men could claim: a 12-inch dick. He had several active restraining orders because of King (his dick's nickname) and he'd probably have to file a few more after tonight. Pleasing women has always come easy to him, but satisfying several ladies at one time, was at the top of his bucket list. After tonight, that task will be checked off. Lost in his thoughts, he hadn't heard a word Xavier said since he picked him up ten minutes ago.

"Leric? Leric are you listening to me? Did you bring you some condoms dude? Because I need all of mine, and I'm not giving any of them out."

"Yeah dude I'm strapped, and besides... your hat's not big enough for my head, feel me? So it wouldn't even matter."

"Man whatever, just hurry up. I'm not in the mood to hear Kara's mouth about us being late and shit. And for your information, you're not the only one sitting wide and hanging low my brother. Know that!" Xavier shook his head and gave Aleric the side eye.

"This dude here. My hat's not big enough for his head...fool please!"

"Whatever you say dude, whatever you say." Aleric said laughingly.

CHAPTER III

Aleric barely put the car in park before he jumped out, because Xavier was working his nerves. Xay had always been giddy over females, but this was just ridiculous. The man wouldn't stop talking about his penis and where he was going to put it. When Jeremy opened the door Aleric damn near pushed him over to get inside.

"Damn Leric, you're about to beat my ass to get in the door ain't you? What the hell?" Jeremy asked.

Aleric flicked his hand at Xavier.

"Man, you just don't know what the ride over here with this cocky bastard has been like. All he talked about was how good he looked, how many chicks he was banging out tonight, how he's about to add some more pretty faces to his stalkers list…blah blah blah… and yada yada yada! I couldn't wait to get out of that car." Aleric said.

"Cocky for what? Boy bye! We all know that the ones who talk the most aren't working with much and do little to nothing in the bedroom. I can't wait to see you crawl at these ladies' feet tonight. I'm going to try and get a picture." Bren said tauntingly.

Xavier was about to say something slick, but he couldn't. His heart got caught in his throat and his big man below started to tingle.

Damn she's fine as shit in that dress! It's barely taming her ass and breasts and thank goodness that it's not, because I want those joints to pop out right into my mouth...

"Xay! Why are you staring at me like that? Boy close your mouth, because you're not getting any of this. You can trust and believe that baby." said Bren in a matter-of-fact tone.

He is looking good though... but then again he's always looking good. He looks just like Allen Iverson with those big brown Puss-in-Boots eyes, and that smooth brown sugar skin. Damn I'd love to kiss his lips... Wait, what the hell? Bren, snap out of it!

"Okay both of y'all were gawking at each other like you want to bone, so would y'all like for us to head to the club without you? asked Chassidy.

"What? Nah man, I'm good. I was just caught off guard because for once she looks like a sexy grown woman and not a broke down Cicero whore." said Xavier.

"If you see a whore in me it's because you are a whore. It takes one to know one honey." She ran her hands along her breasts and continued.

"Humph, so you think I'm sexy huh?" Bren seductively struts towards him.

"How sexy do you think I am?"

He took a step forward, closing the space in between them and lowered his head as if he was going to kiss her.

"So sexy that you might luck up and get a piece of me tonight. You know I love making dreams come true, and we both know you've been waking up in puddles from dreaming about me." Xavier answered.

Everyone laughed except Bren.

"Chile bye! You've probably stolen some of my pictures off of my Facebook page to masturbate to at night. I wouldn't put it past your nasty ass." She said in her own defense.

"Ugh, you two get on my damn nerves! Can we just go now please? Kara interrupted.

"Wait, before we go, let's have a shot of Tequila. I need something to calm my nerves." Jeremy admitted.

Jeremy ran into the kitchen to grab a few shot glasses and the Tequila.

"Bonita Platinum? Man that Tequila is expensive. It's $100 a bottle. Oh shit, I forgot Jeremy got that long money." said Aleric

"A hundred dollars for some Tequila? This shit better work miracles like holy water. As a matter of fact, let's bless the bottle." Chassidy said jokingly.

"Chassidy you're so hood. We haven't blessed a bottle of liquor since we were shorties growing up on Lotus and Wabansia." said Bren.

Jeremy filled all six shot glasses to the top and passed them around.

"Glasses up...drinks down."

Bren held her glass up high and glanced over the group.

PLEASURE PALACE

"Let's toast to a night filled with fun, laughter, and raunchy, nasty, freaky, kinky, X-rated, off the chain, mind-blowing sex. Oh yea, and no slip-ups! Protect yourselves. Clink-clink!"

They downed the Tequila in unison and headed out. Kara could tell that Jeremy was still very hesitant about going to the club, but it was too late to change her mind now. She gave Jeremy a kiss and reassured him that everything was going to be fine before they split up to ride with their best friends.

"Damn he's spooked to let his pussy loose. You must have some gold between your legs girl! Shit, he's looking like he might not get his kitty back. Am I right Kara, or am I just imagining things?" Bren teased.

"Shut up Bren and just drive! My man doesn't have an insecure bone in his body so you can chill out with all of that nonsense." replied Kara.

"Sorry K, but I'm with Bren on this one. He seems uncomfortable as hell going to this club. Don't ruin your relationship trying to prove a point, Kara. Wait a minute, did I just agree with Bren?" Chassidy asked.

"Whatever Chass, and yes you did. Nothing can come between Jeremy and me. We're getting married next Saturday regardless of what happens tonight. Period! Point blank! End of this annoying and meaningless discussion."

"Yea we'll see Kara. We will see." Bren shot over her shoulder.

"It's about time. I'm ready to go. What, y'all had to go over some rules or something?" Xavier asked teasingly.

"Naw man, mind your business. You always have something to say." said Jeremy.

"Leave him alone Xay, damn! Always starting shit!" Aleric yelled.

"He better." Jeremy warned.

"Or what? Don't snap at me because you and Kara are trying to prove Bren wrong when both of you know that she's right. There's no way in hell you two are still getting married after tonight. The guilt and wondering if you both were pleased by strangers better than by each other… things aren't going to be the same between you two and you know it." Xavier said.

"You know what I hate? I hate a person who tries to shit on something that they want. You wish you had a 'Kara'. You wish you had a woman of her stature, a woman to love you and to come home to. You're a jealous ass little boy. You always have been and the shit is starting to really get on my nerves." retorted Jeremy.

Aleric's eyes bucked out of his head.

"Shots fired! Shots fired! Ring the alarm!"

The two men had a brief stare-off in the rearview mirror before Xavier gave Jeremy the finger. They rode the rest of the way in silence. The tension was so thick that a chainsaw couldn't even cut through it. Out of the three of them, Xay and Jeremy always butted heads ever since high school. Aleric had always played the peace maker, but for the first time, he had no idea what to say. Xavier was out of line for what he said, but he wasn't lying. Jeremy was clearly bothered by his fiancée's wanting to do something that will put their relationship on the line.

"Come on fellas, this is supposed to be a fun evening. With our careers and personal lives, we barely get to hang out. I know y'all are not about to bring down the mood with this pettiness. We're boys. Come on now, squash that shit." Aleric demanded.

"Man please with that peacemaker crap. Just a second ago you were instigating talking about "ring the alarm" with your petty ass." said Xavier.

They laughed simultaneously.

"Yo Xay, I'm sor..."

Xavier interrupted.

"Don't worry about it. You my boy, so we're good, and for your information, I do not want a 'Kara'; she's a good girl. I like them bad."

"Thank you! That's what I like see! I'm glad that y'all squashed that because we're almost there. I see the sign." Aleric pointed out of the windshield.

"Chassidy do you see Aleric's car anywhere?" asked Kara.

"Chile you know Aleric drives like a bat out of hell. He's probably damn near there by now. Text Jeremy to see where they are." Bren instructed.

This bitch obviously didn't learn to only speak when spoken to, but I'm going to be cool. She has one more time, though and I'm going to hurt her feelings, thought Kara.

She sent a 'where are you?' text to Jeremy and his response made Bren's prediction correct.

"They're pulling into the parking lot now." said Kara.

"See, I told you. Aleric puts the pedal to the metal! He doesn't play baby!" Bren said laughingly.

"Tell him that we're about five minutes away and not to go in without us." said Chassidy.

"Kara just texted me. They're five minutes away." Jeremy announced

"They pulled off before us, so how did we make it here before they did?" Aleric asked while shaking his head.

"Because women can't drive, that's how." answered Xavier.

Jeremy wasn't impressed by what he saw. The building looked small and dingy. He didn't find anything too appealing about it.

"Bren said this place stays popping. There are a lot of cars out here, but it doesn't look like shit though." said Jeremy.

"I was thinking the same thing. The nicest thing on this place is that big ass 'Welcome to Pleasure Palace' sign." said Aleric.

"Lord please let the chicks in here not look busted and wretched." Xavier said with his hands to the sky.

Jeremy looked over his shoulders before speaking. "Real quick before the ladies pull up, what are y'all trying to get into when we get in there? I'm not trying to fuck, I'M TRYING TO GET FUCKED!" he yelled.

"Oh, look who's exited now!" Xavier looked over at Aleric.

"He's trying to get fucked tonight!"

They all laughed and Jeremy punched his friend in the arm. "Aye, I'm starting to think this won't be as bad as I thought. Now answer the question punk."

"You already know what I'm trying to do. I'm trying to top my sophomore year in college when we crashed that frat party, remember?" said Xavier.

"Yea we remember, because you wouldn't shut up about it. What you had about 3 chicks that night right?" asked Aleric.

"Yep and I'm trying to double that. I'm ready to pass this dick around like a baton! What about you Leric?"

"I just want that one chick to fuck me into a coma. I'm tired of dominating. I'm ready to be dominated." replied Aleric.

"Oh shit chill, here comes the ladies."

"Jeremy please, nobody in that car belongs to me so I'm going to talk about whatever the hell I want to." said Xavier.

"Shut up Xay. We all know that you're secretly praying that you and Bren end up fucking tonight. You've wanted her since college." said Jeremy.

"Naw Bren has wanted me all of this time, and SHE'S THE ONE who's secretly praying to get some of this tonight, straight up."

"Y'all both have wanted each other since forever and I personally hope that y'all fuck each other's brains out so this juvenile bickering between you two can end for good!" said Aleric.

Jeremy and Aleric opened the ladies' doors and helped them out of the car.

"Whew thank you Leric and Jeremy for being such gentlemen. Maybe y'all can school your boy over there on chivalry and what it entails." said Bren.

"How do you get out of the car talking shit? Just get your ass in the club. I'm tired of standing out here." Xavier responded irritably.

"Bren and Xay, can you two please play nice for one night?" begged Chassidy.

Xavier and Bren both rolled their eyes and headed towards the entrance. Aleric shook his head and started behind them.

PLEASURE PALACE

Chassidy wrapped her arms around Jeremy and Kara's shoulders.

"If I get kicked out before I get some dick because these two crazy asses can't get along, I'm going to jail for attempted murder, so get my bail money ready."

CHAPTER IV

There were two huge men guarding the entryway. One of the men looked like a buffer version of Taye Diggs. His smooth dark chocolate skin with the pink lips and square jaw line made him a splitting image of the well-known actor. The other one wasn't so attractive. Unlike the Taye Diggs look-a-like, he was extremely light... almost pale. His eyes were cat-like with the left one noticeably bigger than the right. A long keloid scar trailed from his left eye down the left side of his face.

"Good evening ladies and gentlemen. The fee is $40 to enter and I need to see some identification please." the attractive guard stated.

"FORTY DOLLARS! BREN YOU DIDN'T SAY SHIT ABOUT PAYING THAT MUCH TO GET INTO THIS CLUB!" yelled Chassidy.

"I got you Chass." Aleric went in his pocket and pulled out a c-note.

"Here man, keep the change."

Everyone else followed suit and handed the bouncer their money and ID's.

"Thank you. Everything looks good here. Enjoy your night everybody." The sexy bouncer flashed a set of pearly whites before opening the door leading into the club.

"Excuse me but has anyone ever told you that you look like the actor Taye Diggs? Hi, I'm Bren." she extended her hand.

"I'm Cory, and yes, I hear that all of the time. I think I look way better, don't you think?"

"I agree. Will I see you inside of the club?" she asked.

"Naw, we're not allowed to hang out with the customers, but maybe I'll catch you on your way out."

"Bet. I'll catch you later Cory." She looked over at the other bouncer.

"And what's your name?"

Instead of a name, she got a scowl and an eye roll.

"Ugh, well excuse me for being friendly, gosh." She rolled her eyes and went inside.

PLEASURE PALACE

The room was pitch black with a few strobe lights flashing throughout. There were old dusty looking guys trying to pimp a few wretched looking females at the bar. People who didn't even look like they even clubbed were posted up against the walls watching everyone else get it in. Other clubbers were making out in various corners of the room, and there was the occasional hoodrat group of females on the dance floor twerking to the New Boys 'Freak my shit' song showing everything that God gave them. It was basically your typical Chicago night club.

"Damn does she even have on any panties? Let me go and introduce myself." said Xavier as he danced his way over to the scallywags on the dance floor.

Kara shook her head and laughed.

"That boy is a damn fool! If he even smells some easy pussy he's on it! Let's go get some drinks."

"Yea you're not lying about that, but y'all go ahead, I see something that I like." said Aleric.

PLEASURE PALACE

He had his eyes on a thick high assed redbone ever since he stepped inside of the club. Either she lived in the gym to get her ass that round and high, or she paid some doctor a hell of a lot of money for a banging ass Brazilian butt lift. She wore an off the shoulder skin tight red dress with gold trimming that brought attention to every last one of her curves. The club was dark and he'd hoped that her face was a solid ten like her body was.

"Excuse me Miss Lady. I'd like to introduce myself. My name is Aleric and I noticed you when I first stepped into the club. I was wondering if you'd like to get a drink or two and get to know me."

He almost threw up in his mouth when she turned around and the strobe light hit her face. He didn't know if the basketball star Anthony Davis was staring back at him or the puppet Bert from Sesame Street. He thought that when he made the 'Ooo shit, what the fuck is that?' face, it would deter her from coming any closer, but he was wrong.

"You don't have to look like that baby. I know I'm sexy. I'm Brandy, and what did you say your name was again?"

She placed her hand on his chest and revealed a yellow and brown set of jagged teeth.

"No, fuck that, I'm good. My name is no longer interested. You have yourself a good night!"

He damn near knocked over a few other patrons hauling ass over to the bar.

"Whatever! You don't look man enough to handle all of this anyway! I saw the way you were looking at me. All of this thickness scared you! I don't do punks anyway! Damn! I knew I should've worn the other dress. I've never really looked good in red."

Aleric snatched Jeremy's drink out of his hand and tossed it back.

"Bartender, whatever that was, give me another one!"

"Damn Leric what's wrong with you?! You act like you've seen a ghost, taking my drink and shit." said Jeremy.

"Nah worse. I saw a monster! Man if all of the chicks in here are busted like that broad I just encountered, then I'm good, I'll catch y'all later. I don't do zoo, farm, or wild animals." said Aleric.

Kara choked on her drink.

"Ouch! She was that ugly? Damn Leric, you are bogus as hell."

"Kara you have no idea! Here comes Xay ass. How much y'all want to bet he got some numbers already? Matter of fact, he probably got all of those chicks phone numbers."

"Whew! I haven't done so much bumping and grinding with my clothes on since college, or was that high school? Yo my man let me get a glass of Conjure on the rocks, thanks."

Xavier looked around at his friends.

"Why are y'all hugging the bar? Go get into some shit. Y'all posted up like some lames. This is why I barely hang out with y'all. Y'all act old as hell."

"Just because you stay running laps in some chick every night, it doesn't mean everybody is out here in these streets all of the time. Any who, I'm getting liquored up for when the clock strikes twelve." replied Bren.

Xavier gave her the finger with both hands.

"What's going down at twelve o'clock?" asked Chassidy.

Bren smiled.

"That's when the real fun begins."

"Well until then, we're going to dance. Come on baby." Jeremy grabbed Kara's hand and pulled her onto the dance floor.

It doesn't matter where he's at or what he's doing, when J. Dash's song 'Wop' comes on Jeremy can't help but move.

Bren watched as the couple danced all over each other like teenagers in a basement party.

"Mmm mmm mmm, look at those poor babies. They're happy now, but in thirty minutes the whole dynamic of their relationship is going to change forever and I can't wait either, because Bren loves to be right."

PLEASURE PALACE

"Bren why do you want them to break up so damn bad, huh? See now you're starting to piss me the fuck off..."

Chassidy stepped in front of Bren and folded her arms.

"I really feel deep down that you schemed and plotted this entire thing in hopes that one of them would call off the wedding. Why Bren? I really want to know why you're so hell-bent on proving this messed up theory that their relationship is shallow. Is it because you fucked up your engagement by sleeping with your fiancé's brother the night before your wedding?"

Bren's stomach did a few flips at Chassidy's harsh words.

"Fuck you Chass! This isn't about that okay? And I'm a grown ass woman, so I don't have to explain myself to you or anyone else...seriously."

"Is it not? Your ass is jealous and bitter that our best friend is about to have something that slipped right through your fingers, because you couldn't stop being a slut for once in your life! You bitch...I'm sick of you throwing that negative shit everyone's way because you can't hold on to anything good in your gotdamn life. You hear me Bren, I'M SICK OF IT!"

Without even knowing, Xavier stepped in between the two just in time, because shit was about to get real.

"Uh, what the hell did I just walk up on? Why are y'all mean-mugging each other like that? What just happened?"

Neither woman answered or broke their stare. He took a step back and looked back and forth at his two friends. Bren looked like she wanted to smack the shit out of Chassidy and Chassidy looked like 'bitch try it and see what happens'.

"Aye I don't know what I just rolled up on. All I really want to know is when exactly is the freaky shit popping off? I found a few bad bitches that I plan to run up in when the time comes. Actually, more than a few, but that's none of y'all business." Xavier said trying to lighten the mood.

Chassidy looked at her phone.

"In twenty minutes. I'm going to find Aleric. I'll leave you two hot in the asses alone." She rolled her eyes and sashayed into the crowd.

"Yo, what the fuck is her problem?" asked Xavier.

"You know she hasn't had any real dick since Tupac and Biggie Smalls was alive, so she's testy as hell. I hope she gets ran up in tonight. Maybe it will fix her damn attitude." said Bren.

He was about to crack a joke on her, but instead he grabbed her by the opening on the side of her dress and guided her to the middle of the floor.

"Aw shit! This is B.O.B's new joint 'Headband'."

He pulled Bren closer and pressed his lips against her ear while rapping the lyrics to her.

"Hey, look at baby over there, what's up little mama come here, she started talking but I really couldn't hear, until she started dancing like she do it in the mirror, like she do it in the mirror, like she do it in the mirror, she broke it down started moving like Shakira, like she do it in the mirror..."

She pressed her back further against his chest and locked her wrists behind his neck. They gyrated and swayed in silence to the beat of the track, like they were the only two on the dance floor.

"Look at those two dirty dancing and shit. They make me sick fighting one minute, feeling each other up the next. Those two just do too damn much for me." said Kara.

"Let's just all wish upon a star that they don't catch an STD or crabs tonight okay?"

"CHASSIDY!" Jeremy, Kara and Aleric yelled.

"What, hell? Y'all know both of them are slut buckets! Hot in the ass! New age tramps! And much more! Don't act like y'all don't know that they be out here extra generous with their genitals!" shouted Chassidy.

The music was abruptly replaced with a sultry feminine voice. Xavier and Bren was so zoned out that they didn't realize that they were still holding each other after the music stopped. It was Bren who finally separated them.

"Do I have everyone's attention now?" asked the mysterious voice. A curvy shadowy figure holding a microphone leaned against the DJ booth.

"Can someone behind the bar hit the lights for me please? Thank you ever so kindly."

When the lights came on there were gasps, oooh's and aahh's, a couple of 'damn she's fines', a few 'oh my god', and a handful of 'Jesus Christs'. There was now a sexy face to place with the seductive voice that bellowed through the speakers, and God she was beautiful. She stood at about 5'4, brown skin, with bedroom eyes the color of black coffee. She sported a curly asymmetrical bob that complimented her oval shaped face. Her lips are shaped like Jennifer Gardner's and her body in that white dress mirrored the singer Ashanti. The men weren't the only ones drooling over this black goddess. Even the women had to wipe the slobber from the corner of their mouths.

PLEASURE PALACE

She slowly walked to the middle of the floor and brought the microphone to her lips.

"Hello everyone, my name is Eden, and I would like to welcome you all to my club Pleasure Palace. Every single day at twelve o'clock midnight, Pleasure Palace makes the transformation from a night club to a sex lounge, but sadly, not everyone gets to join in on the fun. You have to pass my tests in order to make it to the lower level into one of the 30 rooms. I like to call the downstairs area The Sex Lounge... also known as Rated R. There are rules, and are as follows: No cell phones, no forceful contact, and no fighting over dick and pussy. There are enough genitals for all of us. Last, but not least... have a good ass freaky time!"

Jeremy tapped Aleric on the arm.

"We should've done more research about this club. Bren didn't tell us shit with her ole funky ass."

"Well hell I didn't know all of this either. When ole girl was talking about it at the salon, she didn't mention any tests. I told y'all everything that she talked about." she yelled.

"Let's start with looks. If you're facially depressed then you have to go. Nobody wants to freak on someone that will give them nightmares for many nights to come. There's nothing worse than being horny, only to have someone's ugliness chase that wonderful feeling away. So if you're ugly, sorry but you have to go! See you later!"

Aleric breathed a sigh of relief when he saw the bouncers removing Brandy and a few other ugly ducklings from the club. That's one thing he and Eden agreed on: sex with ugly people is not his thing even though he wasn't the best looking guy on the planet.

"Now that that's out of the way, I need everyone to strip down to their undergarments. Ladies may keep on their heels, other than that all I want to see are boxers, briefs, panties... or not, and bras... or not." she said.

"What in the world...is she serious?" whispered Kara?

"Um yes I am. I am very serious. Strip down or leave. It's up to you."

Jeremy shook his head.

"You are so damn loud. You could never whisper."

"Shut up Jeremy! I know how to whisper dude."

Xavier and Bren were undressed before everybody, which wasn't a surprise at all, but Chassidy was a bit more hesitant.

"What's wrong Chass? You're taking your clothes off in slow motion like an elderly person." said Aleric.

"Um, I'm getting naked in front of my best friends and strangers, it's a little awkward don't you think?" she responded.

"Nope, I'm pretty cool with it. It's natural and besides, you look good. You have nothing to worry about." he said reassuringly.

Eden began to walk around in a circle examining everyone left from head to toe. She approached the group and lingered. She carefully and intensely ran her eyes up and down each and every one of their bodies, making faces and sounds throughout her examination. She made it to Aleric at the end of the line and smiled.

"What's your name sweetie?"

"Aleric."

"Aleric? What a beautiful name. What does it mean?"

"It means noble, a regal ruler in German." he replied.

"Mmm, a sexy name for a sexy man. I can tell just from your posture that you have a hefty package down there and good stamina. You can go all night and can lead a woman to many orgasms. You sir are a beast in the bedroom."

She stood on the tip of her toes and leaned into his ear.

"It takes one to know one. You are definitely welcomed to stay tonight. Hell I might have to come see you myself later on." Eden gave Aleric's crotch a few little pats and then turned her attention to Kara.

"You look so soft and so pure. I bet that you are extremely sensitive to touch. The lightest kiss, the slightest touch, drives you wild and over the edge. With this pretty little face of yours I bet when you cum, you're gorgeous. I like you, you can stay."

Eden placed her hand under Jeremy's chin and moved his head from side to side.

"God you're gorgeous! Whew ladies do you see this beautiful man here?!" Eden had all of the remaining ladies in the club in an uproar. They were touching themselves, flicking out their tongues, blowing kisses and purring like kittens. The whole place sounded like there were thirty Eartha Kitt's in the room.

"I can tell that you are nothing to play with in the bedroom. You are strong with a lot of endurance. You know how to make a woman beg for it... but you're passionate. Oh yes my love, you most definitely can stay."

"Yea hi, hello there, um what about me, and all of my sexiness." yelled Xavier.

"Ah yes you, Mr. Show off! Mr. Mack daddy! Mr. 'I have hoes in different area codes'. You are quite handsome, that's no doubt, but you're all about being satisfied. I'm not sure if you know how to return the good deed."

PLEASURE PALACE

"Please, that's never a question. I always satisfy… always." he stated in his defense.

"We'll see, but any who... You, Miss Lady is tighter than a wind-up toy. You're obviously in need of a nice hard fuck. With those piercing hazel eyes, I'm sure dick will be the least of your problems in here... and you have pretty feet. I love a woman with pretty feet. You may stay." Eden gave Chassidy's breasts a couple of squeezes before addressing Bren.

"And last, but most definitely not least; you my darling are a bon-a-fide vixen. You know how to pop that coochie and pop it real well. So well, in fact, you probably can be paid to do so. I'm guessing that you're flexible and will try anything. You're stunning and you exude sex appeal. It would be my pleasure to have you join us tonight."

She went on to choose ten more women and ten more men, excluding those with ugly feet, bad hygiene and seemed to be too timid.

"Phase one is complete, now all of you that have been chosen must strip down

to your birthday suits and wear a club towel.
Like I said before, ladies your stilettos are
optional. My bouncers Cory and Shawn will
place your undergarments with the rest of
your things in a safe place."

"Aye Bren, you need some help with
that? You know I'm always down with
helping someone put on their birthday suit."
Xavier tugged at Bren's bra.

"No I have it Xavier. Thank you very
much, with your perverted ass." She rolled
her eyes and handed her things to Cory.

"Once everyone is draped in towels,
come downstairs and I'll be waiting for you
with further instructions. Oh and hurry up, I
don't believe in keeping the horny waiting."
Eden gave Cory and Shawn kisses on the
cheek and a slap on their asses before
leaving them with her guests.

PART II: WELCOME TO PLEASURE PALACE

Deep inside the very core of us,

You will find dark, **forbidden** desires.

Desires that gnaw at our souls relentlessly.

Starving for **passion** and seduction,

The depths of our sexual cravings

Shift us into torrid beasts on the hunt for

impure, immoral, unadulterated sex

In a world where there is one rule and one

rule only:

To **cum** or to make cum

Welcome to **pleasure palace**

Get lost in ecstasy...

If you dare!

CHAPTER V

Shawn and Cory did a sweep to make sure anyone who wasn't supposed to be there was out. They'd caught a few people in the past hiding in the cut trying to sneak to the lower level. The guards locked down the upstairs and led the twenty-six of them to the sex lounge. The atmosphere was completely different. The color of the room and the lighting were soft... and very sexy. Upstairs was filled upbeat music, but now moans and sultry music echoed throughout. From the sounds of things, they were definitely in the sex lounge.

"Sounds like someone has gotten started without us." said one of the guests.

"Not quite. Ms. Eden will join us in just a few minutes, so hold your horses." says Cory.

As if she heard her name, Eden came waltzing out of a room with her dress hiked up around her waist and her lipstick slightly smeared.

PLEASURE PALACE

"Hello again my lovely freaky friends! Are you ready for some sex-filled fun?" she asked while combing her hair with her fingers.

"Okay my loves, as you can see, sitting right in front of you are a couple of hats. There's a hat in the shape of a vagina and there's a hat in the shape of a penis. The cock hat is for the women and the pussy hat is for the men, but ladies if you want to taste the rainbow, then that's your prerogative. I'm not tripping. You will each reach inside of either hat and pull out your destination for the night. Just to let you know, no one will choose the same room; you all will experience different sexual encounters that will be both satisfying and enlightening. Now don't be too upset, but we don't allow roaming the sex lounge for the reason of when I first opened there was an attempted rape and I don't play that stealing cookies out of the cookie jar shit. I had to tighten up the rules. Whatever room or area you choose is where you must stay until you're all satisfied and ready to go. Once you're ready to leave, or if you stay until closing time which is five in the morning sharp, Mr. Cory and Mr. Shawn will politely escort you out. Please make sure you have everything that you came in here with, because you will not be let back inside of the club. Here's a recap of the rules: no roaming the sex lounge, if a woman or man says no thank you and that they're not interested in you or what the hell you are talking about, MOVE ON! No voyeurism unless permitted! Some of my team members who are known as "The Pleasers" might be getting it on themselves, so have some patience and wait your turn. No sticking, licking and sucking unless permitted! I just had to make myself clear on that one. Raise your hand if you didn't understand a got damn word that I just said."

Eden looked around the crowd searching for the one idiot who always has a question.

"Are you off limits too, Ms. Eden? Inquiring minds would like to know." asked one of the ladies.

Eden smiled.

"Darling, if you want to introduce those soup coolers on your face to the ones in between my legs, call my name, and I'll be right there to give you what you need, and that goes for the rest of you. I'm also down for some kinky shit. I invented every freaky position known to man. You better ask somebody!" She licked her tongue out slowly at her inquisitive guest before addressing the group again.

"If there aren't any more questions, you all can line up to choose your fun for the night."

Everyone made a single filed line anxiously awaiting their turn to pick their activity for the night.

"Aye Jeremy looks like two dudes have chosen from the pussy hat man." said Xavier.

Jeremy looked at the two dudes at the front of the line.

"As long as they don't bring that shit over here 911 won't have to be called, because I'm busting heads without a second thought."

"Yo I feel you on that bro, because I'm swinging for the fences." said Aleric.

Bren rolled her eyes in disgust.

Page 71

"You guys are so homophobic. Don't knock something until you've tried it. You never know you might like it more than you thought you would."

"Bren shut the hell up! Just because you're open to fucking anyone including wild beasts, trolls and sewer creatures, does not mean that we all are, okay?" Xavier said.

"Would you two stop it? Bren it's your turn to choose. I'm sick of y'all." said Kara.

Bren gave Xavier the finger and reached into the dick hat. The grin on her face let her friends know that she was pleased with her selection.

"What did you get Bren, because you are cheesing hard as hell." asked Aleric.

She held up her paper and smiled even bigger.

"I'm spending my night in Cocktale Bar. Your turn Chass."

Chassidy's eyes expanded twice its size when she read the small piece of paper. She just knew it had to be a mistake.

"Uh oh, somebody doesn't like what they see. Tell us what it is Chassidy." said Kara.

"The Passion Pit. I'm going to a room called the Passion Pit. Geez Louise, do y'all know what that means?" asked Chassidy.

"Yep! I do!" Xavier said raising his hand like an eager fifth grader.

"That means you're about to get fucked up and down, left and right, forward and backwards, upside down, inside out..."

"Okay Xavier! She gets the freaking point!" shouted Aleric. He stepped around the girls to choose a piece of paper.

"E.R?" he asked puzzled.

"Extreme riding. I think you'll enjoy that room Mr. Aleric, especially since you have a nice saddle to hop on." said Eden.

"Shit I want one of those!" said Xavier reaching into the pussy hat.

"Sexercise? What the hell is this?" questioned Xavier.

"You look fit and in shape, so this should be right up alley Mr. Xavier. As a matter of fact, I think that it's perfect for you." Eden assured.

"It's my turn now, move out the way." Kara took the last piece of paper.

"Aye baby grab mine too, if you don't mind." said Jeremy.

"Let's see where I'm going..." Kara burst into laughter and read hers aloud.

"Sticky Kitty is what I got. What about you babe?"

"Sticky Kitty? That sounds like some off the wall type shit. Let's see, I have... The Suction Room."

"The Suction Room?! Damn! You and Aleric got the good destinations! What the fuck man?!" Xavier said tossing his paper over his shoulder.

"Now that you have your entertainment, go through that black door labeled *Rated R* and just follow the sounds of ass smacking, moans, and dirty talk until you find what you're looking for. It shouldn't be that hard. All activities should be in full swing by now." said Eden.

PLEASURE PALACE

Kara quickly pulled Jeremy to the side to talk to him when everyone else headed for the door.

"Jeremy, I'm starting to have second thoughts. I'm not sure if we should go through with this. I mean is it really worth it? Should we really do this? With it being so close to our wedding honey, this is sort of drastic don't you think?"

"Oh, see now you're thinking like I was thinking at the house a few hours ago. Is it because you've realized that letting Bren talk you into a dare was stupid, or is it because it has finally hit you that I'm about to have sex with another woman?" he asked.

He took the latter as the truth from her lowered head and silence.

"We've come this far, so we might as well prove Bren wrong, right? I mean, unless you think that we're the ones who are wrong? It's up to you honey. I'm down for whatever you decide." said Jeremy.

"No, we aren't wrong at all, and we're not leaving after coming this far. You know what? I'm ready baby, let's go do this."

"Damn what took y'all so long? What were y'all talking about over there?" asked Xavier.

"I know what they were over there talking about? They were talking about if they should go through this door and get fucked by other people or not." said Bren.

Kara was about to curse Bren out but Jeremy abruptly stopped her.

"Nah, we were talking about how wherever you go, we hope that every single dick in that room ends up in your big ass mouth... at the same damn time. That's what we were talking about Bren." said Jeremy.

"Whatever pretty boy. So can we all just agree to meet out front at exactly five o'clock, unless y'all can't hang and want to bail out early?" Bren suggested.

"Agreed, five o'clock in the morning, now open the damn door Bren."

"Xavier, I hope your dick falls off, you community service dick having little boy." Bren threw up the deuces and walked inside.

PLEASURE PALACE

Xavier caught the door with his foot and burned a hole in the back of her head with his gaze.

"God I hate that woman."

"Don't look at me, because I really don't like either one of y'all, now if you'll excuse me, I have to find the people who are assigned to fuck me tonight." Chassidy said squeezing past Xavier

"Chass don't be like that! If you are that in a rush to bust a nut, I'd be happy to make that happen for you!"

Aleric shook his head.

"I guess we should ask for forgiveness now, because Lord knows we're about to do some serious sinning tonight."

PLEASURE PALACE

A **flame** of lust flickers in your eyes

A fire that sends my privates into a fit

Shit...

Disappear into me

As you kiss me into a **frenzy**

Whisper things that are vulgar and kinky

into my ear

I want you to lust me painfully and **bang** me

without fear

Like a **maniac** on crack...

Smack and flip that

Subject me to **delicious** punishment

Weaken me with waves of passion

I'm just asking...

For you to fill me with **fantasies** and

electricity

Forbidden and intense...

Your **tongue** is enticing

PLEASURE PALACE

I smile...as my pussy cries out

From divine **torment**

CHAPTER VI

~THE COCKTALE BAR~

It took Bren no time to find the Cocktale Bar since it was only a few doors down from the sex lounge entrance. A tall topless redhead greeted her at the door, grabbed her by the hand, and led her to a lounge chair with a menu resting in it.

"Hello, my name is Red, and I'm so glad that you've chosen the Cocktale Bar as your sexual experience for tonight. Right in this chair is a menu for you to carefully look over. I'll come back in a few minutes to take your order."

"Thank you Red. I shouldn't take long, but before you go, can I ask you a quick question? And you don't have to answer if you don't want, but are those real? Your breasts I mean... they are just...so unbelievably perky."

She bent down in front of Bren and dangled her breasts.

"You tell me if they're real or not. Go ahead, give them good feel and tell me what you think."

PLEASURE PALACE

Bren accepted the invitation and massaged and squeezed Red's breasts like she was molding play-dough.

"Oh yea they're real alright. These are most definitely real... and soft too."

Bren gave the left tit one last squeeze before letting her server go.

"Let's see what's on the Cocktale menu for the night. Hmmm, this one sounds interesting. The Earthquake is caramel, thick and seven inches... nah I most definitely need more than that! NEXT!"

She ran her index finger down the row of options shaking her head. They were either thick and super short on the inches, or long but too thin. What she needed was a beast... someone who was long, thick, and experienced... someone who would make her slip in and out of consciousness.

"The Savior... chocolate, extremely thick... eleven and half inches... the multiple orgasms and squirt king? Hey Red I'm ready!"

"What are you having tonight?"

"I'll be ordering The Savior please and thank you."

PLEASURE PALACE

"Ma'am I must warn you, many women have left here granted, on their own, but bleeding, limping and hunched over from excruciating pain and well others left in an ambulance. He is freakishly huge in width and length and once he's in there, he has no mercy. The way he has women screaming you'd think they were giving birth, not having sex."

Oh my god is she serious?! Bren pull yourself together, you a grown ass woman! You can handle some dick Chile.

"Um I'm good. He's the one who needs to be worried."

"Okay ma'am if you wish. Mr. Savior will be with you shortly."

Now Bren was nervous. Red had her second guessing her decision in selecting The Savior, and she never in all of her sexual active life, EVER been scared of a penis. Hell she's been fucking since she was twelve years old. After that first taste of the forbidden pole, she never turned back and made it her life lesson to learn how to drive men crazy sexually.

PLEASURE PALACE

Damn Bren you're sweating and shaking like this will be your first time getting fucked. He's not the only one that has sent their lover off wobbly and achy. You know how to put it down too. Remember that...

"Miss, would you like some red or white wine?"

"Huh? Um, I'll prefer to sip on your name all night, and its Bren, not Miss. Thank you Red."

"Red wine it is. I'll have Mr. Savior bring it with him." She gave Bren a nod and went through an unmarked black door.

She was so lost in her thoughts that she didn't notice him standing in front of her. He studied her as she had her head titled back against the headrest with her eyes tightly closed. He ran his eyes from her forehead all the way down to her designer heels. Petite but thick in the right places... she was beautiful and he wanted her...bad.

"Hello Bren, they call me The Savior."

Bren's eyes shot open and landed on an amazon of a man. He is well over six feet with a six-pack and flawless skin. His eyes are alluring... a soft brown like puddles of milk chocolate. The dimple in his chin is small, but deep. His chest and arms looks solid and his hands look soft, but strong. She wasn't sure if she'd made the right decision, but based on how her vagina is beating like a heart against the towel she is wearing, she most certainly had. This man is wickedly handsome.

"Nice to meet you Mr. Savior. May I ask how you acquired your name?"

He handed her a glass of red wine and narrowed his eyes.

"You'll find out soon enough. I must warn you though, I plan to take you to the highest peak of pleasure... to make it there though, you will experience pain; pain that you'll never forget. The Savior is never... ever...gentle.

She swallowed so hard that she heard it.

"And Ms. Bren, I have one little simple rule."
She tossed back the last of her wine and handed the glass back to him.

PLEASURE PALACE

"Oh yea? What's that?"

"You don't cum until I tell you to. If you do otherwise, there will be consequences. Is that understood?

In one smooth motion Savior scooped her off the chair and into his arms. She gasped and wrapped her arms around his neck. He kissed her on hers then carried her off to a dark room with soft music, a variety of lubricants, and a queen sized bed. Lying her down carefully across the bed, he loomed over her; planting two quick, but hard kisses on her throat before standing up. Her thighs were drenched due to so much urgency that she could feel her pussy jumping in excitement. She glared into his stormy eyes as she was barely able to catch her breath from anticipation.

"You're staring at me like you haven't eaten in years. What are you about to do to me?"

He let his silk boxers fall to his ankles revealing eleven and a half inches of rock hard pipe.

"I'm about to fuck you like you've never fucked Bren. Now open your mouth

nice and wide and your legs... open those
even wider."

PLEASURE PALACE

Let's go

Ready to overflow into the depths of **ecstasy**

You enter my precious pond

I push you back and **whisper** "Hold on"

I begin to wind my hips into tiredness

Strokes both cruel and divine

Orgasms rush from our toes to our minds

I watch as the **desire** in your eyes spread

over your face

And you **surrender** to the deepest pleasure

you've ever known

I hope that you **remember me**

As the **shameless creature**

That freed your tortured soul

CHAPTER VII
~ER: EXTREME RIDING~

Aleric roamed the halls looking for his room for longer than he liked. He was anxious and ready to find out if this would be the night that he'd finally bust that long hard raging nut that he'd dreamed of. He was just about to head back up front to ask Eden for directions, when he saw a chick that looked like Buffy the Body in a nurse's outfit. She obviously spotted him too, because she waved for him to follow her, and so he did.

He couldn't keep his eyes off of her ass. She was switching so hard that her ass didn't bounce... it vibrated. She kept peeking over her shoulder and smiling at him, running her hands up and down her ass while giving it a smack and jiggle as she led him to his destination.

Damn I hope that she's the one who's rocking me out tonight. She just don't know... I'd dismantle that pussy.

They finally walked into a room filled with other women who were also dressed in nurse's costumes and a few others just wearing doctor's coats.

"Welcome to the ER Mr. Aleric. Come and have a seat on the gurney in the trauma room and scope out your partner or partners for the night. There is wine, fruits and various chocolates if you're interested. My name is Co-Co. Alert me by pressing that button on the side of the bed when you're already."

He gave her a nod and a smack on the ass before she sashayed away. Every woman in this room was at his disposal. As tempting as it was to have a threesome, he wanted that one she-devil to blow his mind. He was tired of always dominating in the bedroom. It was getting boring and redundant. Boy meets girl, boy and girl have lopsided sex, girl screams, yells, cums like busted water pipes, while boy has to give himself a hand job while girl is knocked out cold and snoring. No, not tonight. Tonight he was going to be put to sleep. Tonight he was going hear sounds come from him that he didn't even know were in him. It was time for him to finally be pleased beyond comprehension.

He scanned the room filled with beautiful women and had a hard time choosing his lover. They all had that video vixen look with the double d cups and large asses and heavy make-up, but then there was *her*. Her complexion was chestnut brown with shoulder length hair of the same color. Her body wasn't trying to escape her nurse's costume like the others, it complimented her curves. Her eyes were small and slanted as if she was of Asian descent. One would assume that she ran track based off of her thick thighs and calves. He loved women with nice legs and lips, and she had both. Her bottom lip looked soft and plump, and he couldn't wait to taste them. Yea she was the one. She had his full attention and he planned on returning the favor. When he smacked the button on the side of the gurney, Co-Co's breasts began to glow. She looked down at the flashing red light and headed towards him.

"Yes Mr. Aleric, you've made your decision?"

"Yes I have..." He looked down at the bulge in his towel and smiled.

"We choose her, with the dark slanted eyes."

"Her name is Jelly. Good choice. She'll be right with you." Co-Co leaned over and softly bit his ear.

"If you change your mind and want double the trouble, let me know."

She gave the rock poking out from between his legs a long kiss and lick before closing the curtain.

"I just might baby girl, I just might."

His dick was trying to break free, so he stood up and paced the floor.

"Nervous?" She stood with hands on her hips and a devilish grin on her face.

"Me? Nervous? Nah, but you should be."

He leaned against the gurney and made his dick hop repeatedly.

"I can appreciate a good challenge. Let's get started, shall we?"

She began to undress without ever removing her eyes from his. Underneath her outfit was an even sexier ensemble. She stood in a two-piece leather chain set. The chains linked across her firm breasts and a chain net trailed from her chest slightly covering her shaved pussy.

"My my my, aren't we sexy... come here."

Slowly and seductively she made her way to him. Jelly smiled at the hint of impatience she spotted in his eyes. Before she knew it, he latched on to her chains and pulled her between his legs.

"Impatient aren't we?"

She slid her hands up and down his chest, making herself wetter.

He flicked her hair from her shoulders and ran his fingers through it. She gasped at his grip, and it made his heart race. Aleric roughly slid his hands down her back and cupped her ass. Jelly pressed her center against his and licked his Adam's apple.

"What do you want me to do? Do you want to feel me? Say yes and watch what I do." She said.

He slid back on the bed and pulled his dick out.

PLEASURE PALACE

"I want you to drop down low on this dick."

PLEASURE PALACE

Dive deep into my sweet abyss

With your **glorious** and frisky tongue

From **delightfully dirty** licks

Leave me skittish, off-balance and undone

Leave me icky, dripping, and sticky

Down below, the most intimate poems are

spit

Robbing the air right from my lungs

With a scandalous **tantalizing** kiss

CHAPTER VIII
~STICKY KITTY~

Kara's mouth hadn't closed since she walked into the Sticky Kitty. The men looked delicious with their glossy chests, washboard stomachs, and handsome faces. The women looked like they came straight out of a magazine or a music video. They were thicker than a snicker and the outfits they wore made their intentions loud and clear: they were prepared to seduce and conquer.

"How are you Kara? Welcome to Sticky Kitty. My name is Thunder. Let me show you where you'll be."

She took his outstretched hand and followed him to the back of the room. There were big screen televisions showing numerous others receiving oral sex. Kara couldn't stop watching. There were three women eating each other out on one screen and on another, two men were taking turns giving a woman head.

"No worries Ms. Kara, it'll be your turn soon. Come with me."

PLEASURE PALACE

Thunder guided her to a big wheel with numbers that spun like the one on the television show Wheel of Fortune.

"Everybody possesses one of the numbers on this wheel. Some of us share a number. You will give it a good ole spin and whatever number it lands on, that's the person or persons you will be with for the night. Are there any questions?"

Did he say or persons? What in the hell am I getting myself into?

She glanced back over at the flat screen with the two men and woman and closed her eyes. She didn't even want to think about if she spun the wheel and ended up with two individuals going back and forth in between her legs.

"Ms. Kara, are there any questions?"

"Yea, how do you know my name?"

"Ms. Eden tells us who we are to expect in our assigned areas." he answered.

"Are you ready?"

She placed her hands as high up on the wheel as she could and spun it with as much strength as she could muster.

PLEASURE PALACE

Please don't give me two, please don't give me two, please don't give me...

"Seven! You're a lucky girl Ms. Kara."

"Am I? Why?" she questioned.

"After your third orgasm, if you're still conscious, you'll know why."

He gave her a kiss on the cheek and smiled.

"Relax, have some wine... you're going to need it."

"Damn is it like that? I mean what does he have...an anaconda between his legs? The suspense is killing me." she said.

"He? You mean *she*? And that anaconda you're referring to is in her mouth, not between her legs."

"She?! I'm getting fucked by a 'she'?"

"You may be disappointed now Kara, but once I'm done... you won't be. My name is Elation. Have some wine, you look stressed."

"It's that obvious, huh? I have my reasons though."

"Yes it is. Nothing to fret over, honestly. I'm going to please you tonight; nothing more, nothing less. While you're at it, have some pineapples and watermelon. Those two fruits make the cum sweeter."

Elation followed Kara to the tray of food and snaked her hand over hers. She ran a slice of pineapple over her lips and sucked the hell out of it; repeating the same seductive action with several cubes of watermelon. She purposely spilled wine down Kara's chin just so she could lick it off. Elation giggled at the lustful, but hypnotized look in Kara's eyes.

"Taste this."

Elation slowly fed Kara the pineapple, licking drops of juice from her bottom lip. She led Kara to a gray Kama sutra chair and stood over her. Elation narrowed her eyes and flicked her tongue out.

"You can fold your arms, rub a lamp three times and make a wish; still another won't eat your pussy like I'm about to do."

PLEASURE PALACE

A tongue that taste like desire and bad
intentions flusters the soul
Dominate me...

I'm yours

Possess me...

Overwhelm me, make me **woozy** me with

sweet torture

Climaxes are in order...

Grab a handful of my hair and **growl** in my

ear

As I **suck and swallow** you into inevitable

pleasure

Your body goes into a **wild tantrum**

Falling victim to a raging orgasm

Salty and delicious

What a lesson to learn...

That **passion** has no limit

CHAPTER IX

~THE SUCTION ROOM: SUCK, SWALLOW, OR SPIT~

Even though he was surrounded by all of these scrumptious looking ladies, he couldn't stop thinking about his fiancée Kara. She could be getting her back blown out right now. Right now some dude could have her screaming to the heavens in an octave he'd never made her reach before. So many fucked up questions and scenarios like: *What if she likes it so much that she'll want to come here more often without him? What if she gets so turned out that he wouldn't be able to satisfy her anymore? What if she really does call off the wedding because some Mandingo dick bastard made her catch the Holy Ghost while he was dicking her down?* Those thoughts were speeding through his head non-stop.

He threw back his third glass of Riesling and brought his eyes back to the other chick he hadn't been able to keep his mind off of ever since he stepped foot in The Suction Room. She was absolutely, undeniably stunning. She was wearing a red vinyl halter teddy with fishnet crotch-less pantyhose that were showing off her body ink of random words like, 'Lick', 'Taste', 'Yummy' and 'Slurp'. Her face and lips were shaped like the actress K.D. Aubert with a pair of Kirsten Dunst dimples. Her jet black hair was styled in an above-the-shoulder bob with a mahogany Chinese bang. Every time she smiled his dick got harder and grew longer. He'd finally had all that he could take.

It was like she could feel him staring at her, because she'd occasionally look back at him and bite her lip. She'd slide her hands down her ass and either grasped her cheeks or gave them a light smack. The women she was chatting with would also cop a feel throughout their conversation. She was teasing him, alright. She lifted her hair up in the back just to show off a tattoo that read 'Suck' in cursive. Justin Timberlake's song *Cabaret* came through the speakers, and she immediately started making her ass bounce and clap to the beat. Apparently the energy between them became too much to ignore, because they locked eyes one final time before they decided to approach one another. The stare off between them was intense as they both wore looks of greed and lust. As soon as she got close enough, she snatched his hand and quickly led him to a secluded area.

The room had a black lamp, a round bed, and a video camera in it. She pushed him onto the bed and slowly walked backwards. Leaning against the wall, her mouth began to water at the thought of having him.

"I'm Dior."

"I'm Jeremy."

"Oh I already know who you are Mr. Jeremy. I also know that you've been watching me all night like a hawk… salivating."

"You haven't been able to keep your pretty little eyes off of me either Dior, so please don't front."

PLEASURE PALACE

"Oh there's no fronting Jeremy. I noticed you the moment you walked in. You're gorgeous... sexy... addictive."

"Addictive? How so?" he asked while massaging his package.

She licked her lips for what seemed like the hundredth time before answering.

"I know for a fact that whomever you're screwing on a regular basis craves you, needs you, and wants you all of the time. Just like the boss lady, I can tell when a man is a beast sexually, and you sir most definitely have something dangerous between your legs."

She walked over to him quickly and pushed open his legs with force.

"I want that in my mouth right now."

She lowered down to her knees and licked his crotch, never removing her eyes from his.

"Please?" she begged while opening her mouth as wide as she could... ready to taste his answer.

PLEASURE PALACE

Passion **boils** and overflows

As the heat between us drags us into lust

Eager and **yearning**

We were forced together by longing...

For a variety of **delicious** orgasms

Orgasms that we wish to feel again and

again

Such a delectable sin...

We explore the **darker pleasures** within

Vivid and explicit...

Our bodies cry out

I howl, you growl

And for one night we'll walk away

breathless...

From love-making that was thrilling and

risky

Through smiles and slow breaths

PLEASURE PALACE

We laugh

Our minds blown by this **erotic journey**

CHAPTER X

~SEXERCISE~

Xavier stood at the door salivating at the women in the room. He had never seen women look so damn good in work-out clothes before. They had on sports bras that looked like if they made one wrong move, nipples would fill the room. They'd probably pop out and put someone's eye out. And the booty shorts; you could barely see the fabric, because it was covered up by so much ass. *These chicks are built!* He thought as he rubbed his hands together like a child preparing to get into some trouble... and that's exactly what he was planning to do.

"Damn these broads in here are sexy as fuck! I'm ready to bang about three of them right now, and I haven't even seen the ones in the back!"

He found his way to a table hosting appetizers and beverages. He hadn't eaten since earlier that day, so he devoured half of the fruit platter and a glass and a half of wine before heading over to a lounge chair with more food to scarf down. A photo of a man and a woman having sex in the doggy position on the left side of the room caught his attention. He began to look around and noticed that every corner of the room had a different photo of a man and woman having sex in different positions. There were lubricants, towels, water bottles, sponges, swings, devices, paddles, whips and handcuffs, and scoring cards spread out all over the stations.

"Oh shit, these chicks are not going to know what hit them. This is going to be too much fun!"

"Indeed it is Mr. Xavier."

"Ms. Lady you shouldn't sneak up on me like that, you might get fucked." He looked up from his plate and into Eden's eyes.

"There's no might about it... I will be. Follow me." She popped her booty in his face.

"Right behind you baby."

He placed his hands on her ass and watched them go up and down like a seesaw from her switching.

PLEASURE PALACE

"Can I have all of you ladies' attention so we can get started? This is Xavier and as you can see he is fine as hell! As most of you ladies know, this is his first time here at The Pleasure Palace, so let's make it a time that he will never forget..."

"Please do ladies... please do."

He was so ready to jump somebody's... anybody's bones that he could hardly keep still.

"Oh no worries Xavier, we plan to wear your ass out! Don't we ladies?!" They all clapped and shouted in agreement.

"You're going to find out just what you've gotten yourself into Mr. Xavier. This group of women have some of the most flexible, deep-throating, acrobatic ladies I've ever had the pleasure of working with and fucking. I can guarantee that you will want to take a little nap before you leave up out of here."

Eden spun around in a circle.

"Am I letting him know girls?"

"So this is how it goes: you get to bang out three women. You have to choose two women with me automatically qualify as the third woman, and then assign us a station. Once you do that, the game starts. The game is called Sexercise: a fuck buddy work-out. The point of the game is to make both women cum within twenty minutes by mimicking the position on the photo in your area. Accomplish that, and I'll be your final and greatest challenge. I've been known to put men in comas with this pussy. I almost always win the nut race. Whoever I'm fucking usually cums first. To be fair, you will have thirty minutes with me. That's if you make it that far. Nothing is against the rules, so you can use your fingers, your tongue and of course your dick. If you make all three of us bust a nut at the assigned times or less, you will be granted free access to the club for an entire month. Do you have any questions Mr. Xavier?" asked Eden.

"Yea, where are the condoms?"

PLEASURE PALACE

We **spiral** out of control
In a **seductive world**

When we play find and lick the pearl

It's dangerous...

But still we **succumb** to

The **craving...**

The thirst...

The **animalism...**

The excitement...

The **hunger...**

The greed...

The **urge...**

The itch…

To be **fucked** into complete and utter

oblivion

Causes our love's below to **drip** with

anxiousness and desire

CHAPTER XI
~THE PASSION PIT~

Chassidy paced back and forth in front of the door that read 'P.P. Orgy Central'. Her palms were sweaty and sweat beads danced on her forehead. She couldn't figure out why she was nervous. It wasn't like she was virgin, but at that very moment she felt like one.

Come on Chass, you can do this. What's the big deal? You were so eager to come here and now you're acting like this will be your first time having sex with strangers. Well it will be the first time having sex with more than one at once, but you've ran through so many dildo's in the past months, so what's the difference? You didn't know them either. Hell you even gave them stripper names so you'd feel less guilty pounding yourself out every other night for the past year. God you're pathetic...

"Are you ever going to go in? You've been reaching back and forth for the doorknob for the past five minutes." A strange voice asked.

She turned around to find a tall, butterscotch colored man. He was built like a professional body builder with piercing green eyes.

"How do you know what I've been doing? Have you been watching me?" she asked.

"Yes I have, but how could I not?"

That response put a big dumb ass Kool-Aid smile on her face, which she immediately regretted.

"Was that a compliment?"

"It sure was, so what's it going to be Miss Lady?"

"Are you going inside?"

He nodded yes.

"Well then I'm going inside. Lead the way."

Chassidy did a double take when the gentleman opened the door. Everyone was butt ass naked and there were moans coming from every single corner of the room. Her mouth dropped open in awe when she spotted a woman with her legs spread wide with some sort of device holding her pussy lips open. It looked extremely painful, especially because of how the man with her was jamming a dildo that looked at least nine inches long in and out, but from the woman's cooing, it was more so satisfying.

"What you're looking at is called the pussy spreader. You place the black circle around the pussy and take the clothespins and clamp them onto your lover's pussy lips. You can penetrate them with anything you want; from a dildo to a vibrator to your fingers… a hand even. It's absolutely up to you. Are you interested in trying it? Oh and by the way, my name Jock."

"Hi Jock, I'm Chassidy, but you can call me Chass, and no, I'm most definitely not interested in that."

"No? Is that more of your speed?" He turned her body so that she'd face a large mat in the back of the room.
She couldn't believe her eyes. The way that his asshole was spread, it was like you could look right inside.

"Now that device is called the doggy style locking spreader. Put that bondage gear on your lover and they'll be locked up like a prisoner. People in here love to get banged out that way. So how about it?" he asked.

The look on her face said *hell no, are you fucking insane,* so he kept at it.

"What about that couple over there? He's using the *take me* thigh cuff system on his partner. The cuffs are Velcro and go around her wrist and her thighs. It's amazing for rough sex."

"Um, no, I think I'll pass on all of those. I'm more of a traditional fucker you know? I'm not into all of this new freaky stuff. I have nothing but a simple dildo at home."

"Well here in The Passion Pit, we experiment and aim to please. Once you're caught up in unbridled ecstasy, all of your sexual fears and restrictions won't exist."

He gently pulled her closer to him and began to slowly loosen her towel. She jumped at his touch. His fingers sent electricity through her entire body. They were soft, warm and strong.

Girl I know you are not getting wet from this man simply tugging at this towel...

shit... I think I better cross my legs...tightly...

As Jock slid his fingers slowly down her belly she crossed her legs and belted out a nervous laugh.

"You seem very nervous Chassidy... no need to be. A few more drinks in you should relax you a bit. We are not here to hurt you; we're here to please you. Your mouth would not have to utter one word, your body will tell us everything that you want and need from us. The body speaks boldly and loudly Ms. Chassidy, did you know that?"

Fighting to keep her balance and unable to speak, she just nodded her head yes. It was like his touch stole her voice.

"Chassidy you are a very very beautiful and sexy woman. Surely you know that... don't you?"

He softly kissed her forehead and then all around her face before lingering on her lips.

"What's your favorite number Chassidy?"

She had to find her breath to speak. She was so turned on by him that she couldn't breathe.

"Six...my favorite number is six. Why?"

He snatched the towel off right where she stood and tossed it to the side.

"Because that's how many of us are going to fuck you tonight."

PART III: COME GET THIS PLEASURE

<u>CHAPTER XII</u>

~BREN~

You slip into me **smoothly**

Like silk pajamas

You lean into me like a **revolving door**

Pushing your way into the depths of me

Your heart is **pounding** with desire

My eyes make you quiver

Your hands make me **shiver**

Baby I'm ready to experience **supreme**

pleasure

I want to lose consciousness from

unspeakable satisfaction

I want you to go down and sip from my

fountain

Taste me…feel me… good and well.

PLEASURE PALACE

Savior was just like the menu described: chocolate and extremely thick. Once she saw his package up close and personal, she knew that her body was about to get rocked. It even looked delicious wearing a condom. He stood by the bed glowering and panting like a wild creature. Damn that was sexy; so... fucking... sexy. His frown deepened. He was obviously not pleased with something, but what? He positioned himself in front of her and leaned back on his knees intensely staring and flexing his jaw muscles. He took ahold of her ankles and kissed the heels of her feet, guiding her legs apart to the width he desired. He glared at her center as if he was angry and then quickly placed his eyes upon hers.

"I want you, but I'm getting the vibe that you're boring sexually, and I don't do boring." He smacked her legs to the side and sat on the edge of the bed.

"What? You have me fucked up. I'm nowhere near boring. I can hang with the best of them. I've never had sex with someone who has the goods that you're working with, but Bren takes on challenges, she doesn't run from them. I don't have a scary bone in my body." she responded.

She sat up on her knees and pressed her chest against his back. Quickly snaking her tongue up the side of his neck; nibbling and sucking on his earlobe. He pushed her back down towering over her in a push-up position.

"I'm going to do things to you that you'll never forget. Your screams will bring the walls down as I'm knocking your walls out. I promise you that."

Using his penis to separate her legs, he pointed to her pussy with it.

"I came to divide and conquer... mmm... I want it. I want that shit. I want it all. Baby I'm coming for that g-spot."

He stretched out completely over her, never shifting his gaze.

"That nut may be inside of you, but for tonight it belongs to me, understand?"

She eagerly positioned her legs on his shoulders.

"Come and get it"

PLEASURE PALACE

He was a beast disguised as a man and she was ready to be his prey. She ran her tongue across his bottom lip then bit it. He played her game and he caught her lip between his teeth, giving it a harsh suck. Not long after her tongue intertwined with his, the two muscles wrestled with hot aggressive passion against one another. His tool was hot and throbbing against her thigh and it was driving her nuts. He roughly slid his hand down her belly and played a beat on her clit with his fingers. She let out a soft moan that let him know to proceed.

"Do you want me?"

She could only nod yes because her center was being played like a drum. He kept circling harder... tapping faster... making her arch her back. Her pussy pulsed against his fingers like a heartbeat.

"Oh no you don't! Not yet. I know what's inside of there is greatly sinful and I'm about to pray on it."

Parting her vertical lips, Savior looked inside; smiling his licked and bit his lip.

"May I have some?"

He ran his tongue up her clitoris as if he was licking an ice cream cone. Licking his index finger, he slowly inserted it into her pussy. Savior roamed her walls as he vigorously licked and sucked her into vocalizing how much she was enjoying what he was doing to her. Just when she thought it couldn't get any better he intruded her moistness with another finger and then another. Frantically moving in and out of her while sucking on her swollen clit like a pacifier, her heart began to race and her moans grew louder.

"You're gonna cum for me? Yes? Give me that nut. Give it to me! I want it..."

And she did... vibrating on the bed as if having a seizure or taken over by the Holy Ghost. Her screams were long and drawn out.

"Uhhhhhh, ooooo shit! I've... never... cum so fast. Never." she said in between breaths.

He licked her cream from his top lip and bit her inner thighs. She jumped from the pinch of his teeth and decided that she'd had enough.

"My turn."

She grabbed his bulging erection with both hands and examined it. *Shit it is juicy and hard as rock.* She took the condom off and gave it a few cat licks and baby bottle sucks before wrapping her mouth around it. She was determined to get as much as she could inside without reaching her gag reflex limits. She learned a long time ago that deep throating could go very wrong if you didn't pace yourself and swallow the inches down.

It went from him running his fingers through her hair, to him gripping and yanking every time she sucked and swallowed.

"Mmmmm, yes baby, keep proving me wrong. Keep showing me that you know what you're doing."

The tighter his grip got on her hair the faster she bobbed up and down. His dick was heavily covered in her saliva, allowing her to treat his cock like a pepper mill. He was starting to push her head down and thrust into her mouth. She opened her eyes to see his joined brows and swollen bottom lip from biting back moans. Savior snatched her up quickly by her hair and slammed her back. He lied on top of her and looked into her eyes. His eyes were filled with ascending desire. His chest felt so warm and solid against her breasts, that she pulled him closer out of greed. There was so much heat between them it was a fucking miracle they didn't burst into flames.

He coated his cock with another condom and then parted his lips making a small entrance for her nipple. His tongue swirled, his teeth nibbled, and his lips sucked until both were hard and tender. He raided her mouth next. The invasion of his oversized tip made her lose the tongue fight they were having. His eyes became slits as he pushed in and pulled out, pushed in and pulled out, resting the tip on her clit, harassing her throbbing pussy.

"You want every inch of this dick, don't you?" He asked knowingly.

Savior folded her legs across his stomach like a pretzel. He took out a couple of inches slowly and shoved back inside with force. He smacked her hands away and scolded her for attempting to push him away.

"Tell me right now how deep you want me to go…" He rammed into her again and again.

"Say it Bren... Tell me to go deeper... Tell me. I need to hear it."

He covered her mouth with his and spoke against her lips.

"I'm going to fuck you until you say my name in the highest octave, repeatedly"

She let out a scream when he melted into her. All eleven and half inches filled her warm moistness making her want to nut right then and there.

"Oh...my...God." she screamed against his lips.

What started off as long rhythmic thrusts instantaneously turned into short stiff strokes. With cruelty, he pounded into her, sending her into an uncontrollable screaming frenzy.

"Fuck Bren. You feel so damn good."

He smiled as her pussy walls convulsed around him.

Page 125

"Remember the rule baby; you don't cum until I tell you to."

He pulled out and gave her pussy an unrelenting spanking. She jerked, cooing with each hard smack.
R. Kelly's "Legs Shakin" filled the room, blending in with her sexual cries.

"Open your eyes and beg for it. Beg for it."

"Please. Please make me cum. I'm ready... God I'm so ready."

The storm in her eyes caused his pulse to amplify. She made him feel like an absolute animal, and he wanted to rip her kitty to shreds. He whispered in her ear, *"Imma make your leg shake"* before plowing into her like a car wreck.

Her insuppressible screams had him on the edge.

"Cum for me baby. Give me that... squeeze those pussy muscles and make your juices spill out all over me. Fuck."

Her right leg started to do a crazy dance, which made him hit her spot even harder.

"Shake...shake...shake..."

PLEASURE PALACE

He sucked in a breath as he sped up, burying his face in her neck to muffle his obscenities. Her body tensed as she screamed in a piercing pitch. Red was pouring herself a drink when she stopped in mid-pour startled by Bren's scream.

"Oh Mr. Savior, I see that you have Ms. Bren in labor." she said to herself.

He could feel himself nearing that place of ecstasy, so he pulled out and flipped her over.

"I'm nowhere near done with you yet. I want to see you jiggle that ass while I hit it from the back."

"What? You didn't cum?" she asked over her shoulder.

"I cum when I'm good and ready. Why, are you sexed out? I'm looking for nut number three from you."

"Well I want to get on top, so let me."
She tried to lift up, but he pushed her face into the sheets.

"This is my show and I want to fuck you from behind, now behave."

PLEASURE PALACE

I guess he didn't believe her when she said that she enjoyed challenges, because the look of surprise on his face when she used her ass to bump him backwards was priceless. She scrambled to straddle him before he could regain his balance. Sitting on his lap, she placed her hands on his chest with force to hold him down. She made the mistake of lifting up to guide his member inside of her, because he used that opportunity to get her on her back. She laughed and bit his chin which ignited a fire in his eyes. They rolled around playfully wrestling like siblings for control. When he growled and swore in her ear, she knew he was angry, and that made her libido hysterical. She laughed and surrendered to the beast.

"I'm going to pound you until sweat rolls down your back, through the crack of your ass onto my dick."

He pushed her head down and entered her roughly as punishment for defying him and got to work. Their bodies went crazy; violently crashing against one another.

PLEASURE PALACE

"Throw it back. Throw that pussy. Don't hold back baby... oooo shit."

Pleasure and pain were both at a high. She pushed back as much as she could without screaming out in agony. He was just so big. She was pissing him off though. He wanted his balls to bounce off of her pussy while he hit it. He smacked her ass so hard that it sent a shock throughout her entire body.

"I said don't hold back got damn it! Fuck me back Bren! Pop your ass harder and fuck...me...back!"

She took a deep breath and complied. She wanted him to remember her just like she will remember him.
Her breasts, with each turbulent thrust, made a slapping sound against her drenched skin, which turned him on.
A wave of pleasure was fighting to take over the both of them and neither of them could hold it any longer.

"Look at me Bren."

He wrapped her hair around his hand and yanked her head back. For the final climax their mouths connected. He stole her breath along with the hardest orgasm she'd ever felt. Her entire body vibrated from the force of her orgasm. It was like a pipe burst the way she came all over the sheets.

"I can't stop cumming. I just...can't...stop...shit."

He closed his eyes tightly and trembled fiercely.

"Fuck Bren! Fuucccckkkkkk!" The room echoed their screams as they collapsed in exhaustion. The orgasms they experienced were so powerful that even after a couple of minutes they were still reaching for air and shaking. She rolled over to face him.

"What's your real name?"

With a bit of hesitation he answered.

"Pierre. You know I must say Bren, you are the first woman to make me call out her name while I'm busting."

"And I believe that you are the first man who may have bruised my intestines."

"Well that's too damn bad, because I want more."

He grabbed her face and held it tightly. He wanted to make her cum until the sun came up, and that's what he planned to do.

<u>CHAPTER XIII</u>

~ALERIC~

Speak to me of how I make your **heart**

throw tantrums in your chest

Of how my eyes touch the very **core** of you

Speak to me of how your passion flows

deeper than the seas

Speak to me of how you need me to want it

Of **how you need me to need it**

Of **how you need me to scream it**

Of **how you need me to feel it**

In a place no one else has ever **touched**

PLEASURE PALACE

Jelly swayed and groped her body to the sounds of Ciara's body party. She could tell that sexually, he is an impatient man, and she wanted to do whatever it took for him to lose his temper inside of her pussy. She was like a gymnast. Balancing on one foot while making her knee touch the side of her face: twirling, dipping... popping her vagina on handstands.

"Yes baby, pop that pussy." he said while stroking his thick tool.

She was starting to get to him. He looked frustrated, annoyed even, but she wasn't going to stop teasing him until he demanded her to. The more she twerked her ass, the faster he stroked himself. He'd finally had enough.

"Come get this dick right now. Oh, and leave the heels on. I want to fuck you in them."

She willingly obeyed his command and slowly crawled onto the gurney. The sexual tension between them was so thick that you would need a chainsaw to cut through it. His eyes were dark and cloudy, full of lust and mischief. She removed his hands and took his fullness in her mouth. She handled his cock like a Popsicle… slurping, plopping, and licking it from the balls to the tip. Sucking and riding dick was her specialty and she was about to unleash all of her skills on him. His rolling hips and her neck action joined together in rhythm. She bopped, he pumped, she sucked, he thrust... deep, hard and fast. He tugged on her hair until she came up for air.

"Give me that pussy. I want it now."

"You want it?" she asked knowingly.

She seductively licked her lips and lowered her body down on his dick into a full split.

"I'm going to grind you until you feel it in your mind."

He arched one eyebrow.

"Relax and let me show you how nasty I really am."

Normally he would question a woman if his hefty package just slid right in, but she felt so good that he dismissed the fact that her warm moistness granted him such easy access. Besides, she worked at a sex club, so she was bound to be a little loose.

Her inner sanctum was so hot and gooey that he wanted to fuck her like he was Speedy Gonzales, but at the same time he wanted to savor every hump between them. She threw a smile over her shoulder and went to work. Her ass cheeks played double-dutch on his lap, bouncing one after the other as she rode him backwards. He smacked her ass like an addict looking for a vein to shoot up.

"Fuck!"

He banged his head against the gurney. She was good. Too damn good.

"You like it daddy? Do you want me to slow it down or speed it up? Talk to me."

"Don't you change a thing baby, keep doing what you're doing. Shit."

She popped up and slammed back down over and over and over again. He couldn't take it anymore and she knew it. His cock was throbbing hard inside of her, but she wasn't about to let him get off just yet. His eyes shot open when she climbed down. The flames in his eyes and the growling in his chest let her know that he was wobbling on the edge, ready to fall into unfathomable ecstasy.

She spit in her hands and rubbed them together. Jelly massaged his penis like she was rubbing in lotion. He let out a low moan which was her cue to devour him again. She kissed it, licked it, kissed it and licked it some more.

"Shit, you turn me on." he confessed.

"Do I? Tell me that you want me. Tell me that you need my pussy to make you cum. Tell me that you want it all."

"Damn baby, I want it all." He muttered hoarsely.

She squatted over his shaft and kissed him recklessly. His tongue found its way down her throat just like his dick did and she sucked it silly. Jelly pushed him back and caressed her entrance with the tip of his cock. He teased her by making his dick jump against her pussy lips like a finger thumping a melon. Within the cradle of her thighs, his penis head played ping pong, sending shocks through her vagina.

PLEASURE PALACE

She threw her head back in pleasure when he filled her with his long thick shaft.

"Goodness daddy, I feel you all up in my belly. Just promise me that you won't cum without me. Do you promise?"

"Teamwork baby, we're in this together." he said while smacking her on the ass.

He grabbed her by the waist and latched onto her nipples sucking them into stiffness. She locked her fingers together in her hair and bounced up and down in a tantrum. Her loud moans brought the monster out of him. His hips gyrated to match her pace, at the same time lifting her up and slamming her down on his lap with force. Got damn she rode it like she stole it. Their lower halves banged insanely drawing out sounds of satisfaction that could no longer be held back within them.

The look of desperation on her face drove him to bang her fearlessly with every ounce of strength that he had. His dick was good, but her shit was too. Her pussy was so good that it had him making the ugliest faces.

"Baby! Shit! I'm about to cum!"

She rested her elbows on his shoulders and locked her fingers behind his head.

"Go a little deeper. I can feel it Aleric... take us home..."

He hugged her and sped up. She was screaming in agony, but he was zoned out, he needed this nut to be a hard one; he wanted her to gush all over him. Aleric didn't want her to cream, he wanted her to squirt, and what he wanted is what he got. Her pussy muscles squeezed his pulsating dick letting him know that she was there. Soon they were consumed by pleasure.

"Oh My God Aleric! Oooooo shit!"

"Ahhhhhh shiiiitttt!"

Never breaking their embrace, they shivered in each other's arms breathless and light headed. In the curves of her neck he whispered a few more obscenities in between kisses. He placed her on her back while still inside of her and searched her eyes.

"You should give classes on how to ride dick. I've never had my dick squeezed so hard like you just did in my entire sexual career."

"Now don't get yourself sprung Aleric. That would be bad for business and teaching classes may not be such a bad idea."

"So what's next?" he asked.

She smiled and put both of her legs behind her head.

"I rocked your world. Now it's time for you to rock mine."

Without hesitation he buried his head between her thighs like he was deep sea diving. She was nasty and it made his manhood twitch. He was going to swim deep into her sea and pull out as many high notes and orgasms as he could.

CHAPTER XIV

~KARA~

Loving you

Pleasing you

Serving you

Is the **sweetest slavery**…

So you'll never forget me

Make me your **greatest memory**

I'm not afraid to **kiss** the depths of your soul

To create a **fire** that burns so cold

To await the expression of your desires

Such a pleasing **sensation**

The tip of my tongue awakens your **body**

I'm not afraid to press **greedy** kisses over

your chest…

To **bite** your neck

PLEASURE PALACE

To whisper, "It's all yours"

Intoxicating

A **tasty** delight

This passion could be the death of us

I'm your greatest **pleasure**

Our **bodies** are so good together

What we have could never be forgotten

I'm asking

Make me your **greatest memory**

So you'll never forget me

"Wow, you don't hold back do you?" questioned Kara.

"No, and you're about to see that firsthand. Follow me please."

Kara went with the sexy vixen through a door with a sign that read 'Sound Proof' at the top. She wanted to ask Elation if that meant what she thought it meant, but decided against it. Moans filled their ears as they passed by different doors. Some were closed while others were open. Against her will, the sight of others performing oral sex was making her all hot and bothered. They were chowing down like it was the Last Super, and their victims were shaking like they were being electrocuted. One chick snatched a patch out of the other chick's head when she climaxed. Another chick had her legs wrapped so tightly around the guy's head she could've suffocated him.

"Oh my." Kara muttered.

"Patience my dear, you're next."

Elation grabbed Kara by the hand and pulled her into a small room with only a stereo and a Kama sutra chair stationed in the center. She watched Elation as she bent over and revealed her bald pussy to her. She pressed play and *Sex Slave Ship* by The Flying Lotus blared through the speakers. She slowly took off her robe and danced her way to Kara. Kara did a double-take. Elation was not only beautiful, but she was dangerously sexy. She was wearing a midnight prowler body suit with a hood, open crotch-less panties, and a cleavage-baring scooped neckline. She had always been strictly-dickly, but fuck it... this broad looked delicious.

Elation drew Kara close to her with force. Her kisses were hard, warm and aggressive, and Kara's knees threatened to buckle under every last one of them. She couldn't believe how weak this woman was making her. Not even a man had ever made her feel this vulnerable... this... horny.

"I'm going to lick it until you can't handle it. That's when I'll know to suck it and bring you on home."

A lump lodged itself in Kara's throat and a million butterflies fluttered inside of her stomach. This was all new to her, being touched by a woman and wanting to be touched by a woman. She was confused but curious. She was nervous but uncomfortably excited.

She laid Kara back on the chair and sat between her legs. Her lips were so succulent and soft Kara couldn't help but to kiss her back deeply...hungrily. Their tongues teased one another... switching speeds and playing peek-a-boo while driving the temperatures of their bodies to smoldering heights. Kara found her hands wondering along her pleaser's body. She wanted to pull them back, but her pussy said *no, touch her... feel her... caress her.* She lowered Kara's towel and wasted no time licking and sucking her nipples like they were ice cream cones melting under the heat of the Sun. It felt so good. She felt so damn good. She grabbed the sides of Kara's thighs and pinched them quickly. Kara knew that this was it. She knew that Elation was about to dig into her, and there was no turning back.

"My serpent tongue is going to slither inside of your Eden until your body cums. Now open those pretty legs of yours so I can explore your garden."

She used her middle and pointer fingers to probe the walls of Kara's pussy. Kara's bottom lip throbbed and swelled from biting down on it every time the tips of Elation's fingers grazed her sweet spot. She slowly removed her fingers and placed them on Kara's lips as if telling her to hush.

"Taste yourself."

She opened her mouth and allowed Elation's fingers to creep inside. Closing her eyes, she sucked on her fingers like a hard piece of candy before releasing them back to her.

"I taste sweet." Kara said with a smile.

"I never take the word of others. I always have to find out for myself. Lie back and enjoy me."

She parted Kara's pussy lips and French kissed her clit. It turned Elation on that Kara was so sensitive to touch that she moaned along with her. Her tongue danced inside of Kara: gliding...twirling...twisting along her walls furiously, and provoking soft gasps and long sighs. Elation used her tongue as a tool to scribble all over Kara's slippery center. Her tongue dashed in and out of Kara's tight hole in a frantic rhythm.

"Mmmmm, Elation you're going to make me cum."

Elation slid two fingers in and flicked her tongue hard and speedily over Kara's clit. The moans heightened. Kara used Elation's ears like handle bars and attempted to take control of the pace. She was ready to explode, but her pleaser had something else in mind.

"Wait! Oh my God why did you stop? Don't stop!" Kara begged.

Elation giggled and spanked Kara's swollen clit.

"Good orgasms come to those with patience my love. Now stand up and sit on my face."

Kara complied and switched spots with her. She wasn't even fully in position before she felt Elation's tongue roaming her pussy. Kara hula hooped on Elation's face and rode her tongue like it was a dick.

PLEASURE PALACE

"Yes baby ride me, and bounce that pussy on my tongue. Let yourself go Kara."

Kara's thighs tightened around her face and allowed her to taste her deeply. Elation's tongue had mad handles and she wanted her to lick her clean. She sucked Kara relentlessly... smacking her ass cheeks with one hand while finger fucking her asshole with the other. Moans of pleasure escaped from Kara's body consecutively. Each one sounded deeper and longer than the one before. Kara tightly hugged herself and moved back and forth like she was in a rocking chair; pumping her pussy at the same speed of her pleaser's wet darting muscle. She began to tremble and stutter. *Lord, her tongue must be from the depths of hell... Dear God, I'm on fire.* Firm and stubborn, Elation's tongue pressured Kara's clit until she filled her mouth with cream.

"Oh fuck! Fuck! Ooooooooo!"

Kara fell forward searching for air to breathe. She had never experienced such a powerful orgasm from oral sex before. It was the best she ever had. Elation was the best she'd ever had.

"You came hard mama, how do you feel?"

Kara laid on her back and pulled Elation on top of her.

"I feel amazing. This just made me realize that all of these years I've been busting mediocre nuts and that kind of pisses me off."

They laughed simultaneously.

"Would you like to taste yourself once more?"

Kara nodded and they shared kiss after kiss, stoking a fire between them that they were both eager to burn in all night.

CHAPTER XV

~JEREMY~

I've never felt so **animalistic**

You own me... don't you know?

Pleasingly plump and sweet

As I savor your sugar cane

The **sound** of you fills the air

Your moan is more than I can bear

I've never felt so **sadistic**

You control me... don't you know?

I want to **sip** from a deep well of desire and

greed

Longing and need

Don't you know... you've won me?

PLEASURE PALACE

He helped her to her feet, and immediately his hands disappeared behind her blouse. He caressed, tugged, and pulled while his tongue played inside her ear.

"Not yet. I want to watch you play with yourself. Put on a performance for the video camera."

"Your wish is my command daddy."

Dior took her orders and ran with them. She faced the recorder and snatched open the snaps sheltering her vagina. She gave her pussy one tap, two taps, and three taps before squeezing it in her hand. She walked over to the bed and slowly lifted her leg above her head. She licked and sucked her middle finger repeatedly, trailing it down her tongue slowly; never taking her eyes off of him. She jammed her finger inside of her center and brought the juices up to her clit. She continued that act gradually increasing the speed of the motion and making her clitoris glisten with her wetness. She tasted herself and moaned as if she was the best thing she had ever tasted.

"Mmmm, yummy."

She inserted four fingers into her mouth, pushing them in and out several times before wiping them off on her pussy. It was like she was cleaning a table or washing windows the way she circled her fingers against her sweet spot. She leaned her head back zoned out in a fast paced rhythm. Her moans were too forceful to fight back as her legs began to shake.

"Yes baby, make yourself cum. Fuck. I want you to cum nice and hard." he said while stroking himself.

Her shaking became stronger and her chest poked out as if she was being resuscitated.

"Ooooo say that again. Tell me to cum again and I will."

"Give me that cream Dior. Let me get that nut."

She threw her head back and shuddered. Screaming and shaking madly, she toppled onto the bed smiling and out of breath.

"Now it's your turn."

She stood up and put her hands on her hips.

"Stand up. Now."

If her tone wasn't convincing, the look on her face said that she meant business. He followed instructions and got on his feet. She walked seductively towards him, biting her bottom lip and circling her nipples with her thumbs. She placed his aching shaft in the palms of her hands. Long and thick... Dior salivated as she watched it throb in her grasp. It looked heavenly and she wanted to taste every inch of him. She bent down and brought the tip to her mouth, patting her tongue with it again and again. She dropped to her knees as if receiving some sort of devastating news and pushed him into the depths of her throat. She began to suck him deep, hard and fast.

He cursed and groaned over and over...thrusting into her...grabbing her by the back of the neck. His balls bounced off of her chin like a paddle ball at full speed. She was a professional and he was guiltlessly enjoying her skills.

"Shit girl you know what you're doing? You're taking all of this dick like a pro. Fuck."

She giggled and slowly pulled out his dick. She coated it with wet hot kisses and rolled her tongue like a roller coaster up and down his big bulging cock.

"A professional? I created this shit. Now, you know what I want you to do for me daddy?"

He sat the head of his dick on her lip.

"What's that baby?"

"While I finger fuck myself, I would like for you to fuck my throat nice and deep. I'm a little parched and I need my thirst quenched with your seed. Can you do that for me daddy?"

"You thirsty baby?" he asked teasingly.

"Very."

She opened her mouth and took him in full, her mouth tightening around his dick like a vise-grip.

"Ooooo fuck! Mmmm!"

She was talented. She moved her fingers up and down her center like a washboard, never losing her rhythm of bopping with his thrusts. He pumped into her mouth completely oblivious to the gurgling and choking sounds she made. He was zoned out.

Dior opened her eyes and watched him throw his head back in satisfaction. His low growls were becoming more frequent and she knew that with just a little more pressure, he would soon be howling like the animal he was. His groans were becoming clearer... louder... he was almost at that beautiful place. She closed her eyes tightly and squeezed his dick as hard as she could to bring him on home.

"Shit Dior! Damn baby! I'm cum...I'm cuming...shiiiittt!"

PLEASURE PALACE

Jeremy shot his hot cream down her throat, grimacing when she sucked him dry. Dior... she led him into beastlike, brutish ecstasy. He was still so turned on that he picked her up, threw her on the bed and proceeded to return the favor. He was a derelict and she was his long awaited feast. He licked all up and through her pussy lips, using his tongue to explore her sticky walls. She purred like a kitten. He inserted two fingers and worked them in and out while sucking the life out of her clit.

"Jeremy, stop! I can't take it. Fuck! I can't take it."

He didn't listen. He watched her squirm and try to push his head away. He kept on and worked her pussy out with no indication of stopping until he got what he wanted. She wasn't the only one good at collecting nuts. Her legs began to twitch and her moans sped up. He coaxed that nut to come out.

"Jeremy!"

She pulled his face deeper into her as she creamed his tongue. Even after she climaxed, he continued to kiss and tug, making her quiver at his every touch. He kissed her inner thighs and lied beside her.

"That was amazing Jeremy. Oh my God I can't even..."

He laughed.

"You're pretty amazing yourself."

"Why thank you very much, but um, I hope that you have some endurance."

"I do, why?"

She rolled on top of him and trailed kisses down his body.

"Because I'm not full yet. I need more of you Mr. Jeremy; ooo wee! Much more."

CHAPTER XVI

~XAVIER~

Confessions and desires

Rip our souls without warning

Our **bodies** are in mourning

Crying out to be **resurrected**

Tired of being lonely and **horny**

Cum for me...

Shape me... mold me into the perfect

orgasm you see...

If I cum for you and you cum for me

We will be reborn within **waves of passion**

inevitably

Leaving our tongues happy and our cores

sweet and dirty

PLEASURE PALACE

Xavier carefully scanned the stations for the activity that he knew that he'd easily excel in. Not that he couldn't make them cum any and every kind of way, but since he was being timed, he had to be smart about his picks.

Hmm let's see here... The Bandoleer position is boring and traditional. If we do The Grip position, I'd be doing all of the work and that definitely can work against me. The same goes for The Sphinx and Clasp positions, so nope. The Glowing Juniper and The Triumph Arch just look weird. Ugh! What to choose what to choose! He thought.

"Okay these are my decisions: I want shorty over there with the pink lace one-piece on to go to The Plough station. I want Miss Chocolate Drop who looks like Foxy Brown to post up at The Indian Handstand station, and you Miss Eden, I would like for you to wait for me at The Lustful Leg station please."

PLEASURE PALACE

"Nice choices Xavier. Like I said, there's absolute freedom to act spontaneously with your partner.
The rest of you ladies know what to do. Just sit back and enjoy the show."

The chosen ladies waited at their assigned areas rubbing and touching on themselves in anticipation of what was to come. He pulled out his stiffened penis and stroked it. Did he want to start with Chocolate Drop or Pink Lace? He'd let his dick decide.

"My dick eagerly pointed in her direction, and it chooses you..."

He walked towards the Foxy Brown look-a-like stroking and waving his dick at her.

"Are you wet for me baby or do you need some assistance?"

She sat back in the chair and slowly parted her knees. Eden sat the timer at the station before addressing the group.

"Okay Xavier you have twenty minutes or less to make her do the Stanky Leg. On your mark...get set...GO!"

PLEASURE PALACE

Xavier lowered to his knees and immediately explored her wet crevice after parting her pussy lips frantically. His tongue moved along her juicy opening like a race car. He was swerving, switching speeds and hitting the walls. His tongue was massive and strong, and he knew damn well how to use it. Her thighs became earmuffs as they closed around his head tightly. He peeked up at the clock and it hadn't even been five minutes and she was already squirming like crazy. He stopped abruptly and pulled her out of the chair.

"Get on your knees and lean on your elbows in the chair."

She ran her tongue across his bottom lip and did just as she was told.

"Mmm, taste like peaches. What's next baby?"

He answered by lifting her hips and penetrating her from behind. She let out a loud gasp and braced herself. He was a normal length but meaty, and he rammed into her like he was neither. She was looser than he liked but that wasn't going to stop him from getting the job done. He went in and out of her like a bulldozer knocking down a building. Long and hard strokes had her hitting notes like Minnie Riperton. The spectators in the background were cheering him on, yelling for him to fuck her brains out. That was the only good thing about this fuck. He couldn't wait until he got to the other chick, because Chocolate Drop was boring as hell. She wasn't throwing the ass back, winding her hips, making it clap or anything.

Her walls started tightening around him, so he kicked it into high gear. She shrieked and laid her head down in the chair. He looked over at the clock and it was fifteen minutes on the dot. He caught the towel tossed by Eden and wiped himself down.

"Whew wee ladies! Mister Xavier is working with a nice package, and he has some power in it. I hope that you're not tired Xavier, because you have two more pussies to raid." Eden teased.

"Tired? Please, she was a piece of cake. You need to be asking Pink Lace if she's ready, because I'm about to act a gotdamn fool in that pussy. Now set the clock Eden." he responded

He took a swig of red wine and grabbed a fresh condom. Eden blew him a kiss and pressed the start button.

Pink Lace pushed him onto the Kama sutra chair and lowered down to his sex. It was still hard, because he hadn't cum. She delicately drizzled a few drops of honey from his navel to his balls and licked it off as quickly as she applied it. She placed one foot on his shoulder and poured honey down her belly, letting it drip between her pussy lips. He cuffed her ass and brought her sweetened pussy against his mouth.

"Oooooo...mmmm"

She tossed her head back and enjoyed him sucking her clit like a lemon. He sucked, and sucked, and sucked until it became plump, throbbing and extra juicy.

"Get into position."

He stood up and gave her pussy a few love taps with the head of his dick. She giggled like a school girl and got down on all fours. She hunched her back like a cat on the attack and jiggled her ass in the air. He grabbed her hips and tucked her legs under his arms when she went up for a handstand.

"Oh Xavier, you'll need to use all of your strength for that position. Are you sure you'll be able to hold it until you get that nut?"

He looked over his shoulder and smiled.

"Watch me."

Xavier busted into her hole like the DEA at a drug house. He waited no time to drill her with short hard thrusts. Pink Lace's moans were turning everyone on. Her soft cries and animal-like grunts had all of their pussies leaking. The ladies in the background broke out into an uproar. They were clearly 'Team Xavier', and it was starting to make Eden uncomfortable. He undoubtedly knew how to please a woman, but he suddenly became some actual competition for her.

He saw that it was already over ten minutes and she still hadn't cum. He was starting to feel it so he had to knock her pussy out.

Page 163

"Stop holding that nut baby girl. You know you want to let go."

He put the pedal to the metal and worked her ass out. She was screaming so loud that her voice was cracking. She smacked the floor and yelled every obscenity she knew before squirting all over the place. His entire lower half looked like he'd just stepped out of the shower.

"Looks like that was pretty close Xavier. From the look on your face you were about ready to spill that seed."

She laughed and ran her finger along the stop clock at her station.

"You won't last five minutes with me."

"Shut the fuck up and throw me another towel and condom."

The whole room said *damn* and looked back and forth between the two. They'd never heard anyone talk to Eden that way and it was an obvious surprise to her, too because her mouth dropped to the floor. She was angry and turned on at the same time and she didn't like it. *Who in the hell is talking to? I know he's not talking to me like that in my establishment?* She was about to show him who was boss like she did with all the rest. She threw the towel with force to let him know that she didn't appreciate what he said. He knew he'd gotten under her skin and planned to use that against her. When he was fucking the other two women, he'd occasionally look over his shoulder and catch her fondling herself, biting her lip, or shivering. She wanted him and he was about to proudly fuck some years off her ass. He lied down on floor and flexed his chest. Narrowing his eyes, he palmed his dick.

"Let's go Eden."

She started the clock and crawled slowly to him. She placed one leg on his shoulder, wrapped her arms around his neck and leaned back. He grabbed her by the hips and entered her gently. They let out moans of passion in unison when she submerged his dick in her pussy. He stilled inside of her and brought his lips to hers. They lay kissing and exploring each other's mouths with undeniable hunger.

"Don't behave; I want you to get disorderly all up in this pussy."

She kissed him before guiding him deeper inside of her.

"Give me that horny creature within you. I want to feel every dirty thought you've ever had."

Her nibbling and sucking on his neck sent his pulse into overdrive. She felt so tight...so warm...so moist. The feeling was electric. It was like voltage running through his skin. He was driving into her with every ounce of strength he had. She was pumping at the same pace as he was, making it harder to hold his release.

"God Xavier! Give me more! Yes! Faster! Harder! Yes!"

Every breath she took was becoming urgent.

"Fuck not yet! Shit!" Thick cream spilled from her core onto his shaft.

He sucked her neck to smother a moan. It was so deep and hoarse that it filled the room. They laid there hugging each other like long lost friends trying to catch their breaths. This was the first time either of them had been mutually satisfied. They burst into laughter and high-five'd.

PLEASURE PALACE

"You got me in ten minutes Xavier. That's a world record. Look around. All of the ladies want a piece of you now. Ain't that right?!"

"Well you won fair and square since you made me climax faster than I ever have. You now have a month of free access to the nightclub and the sex club. Let's give Mister Xavier a hand!"

He took a bow and plopped down in one of the chairs.

"I'll only accept that offer if I can have you for the entire month. Deal?"

Eden straddled him and bit his lip.

"That's only a deal if I can get dicked down one last time before the club closes."

"Deal baby girl... that's a deal."

<u>CHAPTER XVII</u>

~CHASSIDY~

Abandon yourself

Before I

Capture your

Desires

Eyes that set you on

Fire

Good loving that will take you to the sky

and **higher**

Such an

Impassioned

Journey

Kinky thoughts make you horny

Let your destination be inside of me

Munch on my

PLEASURE PALACE

Neck

Open my legs

Play with it

Quaff from my vagina

Rapid tongue movement

Slurping every drop, mmm

Taste my pleasure you've

United our bodies

Viciously pounding me, I'm

Winding my hips with yours

X-rated images we've painted

Yelling you can have it as much as you want

Zillions of times and more

Chassidy stood stiffer than a corpse as Jock ran his big masculine hand up and down her vagina.

"Come with me so we can unleash those orgasms that you've had tied up for so long."

They locked fingers and walked to a secluded area in the room. It had a large circular bed with honey, chocolate, whipped cream and wines surrounding it.

"If you look to your right, you will find jumbo flash cards of the alphabet hanging on the wall. You will choose six letters. Those six letters will represent the initials of the pleasers you'll be spending the night with. Once you choose your letters, I will retrieve those individuals and the time of your life will begin; any questions?" Jock asked.

"Yes, what if more than one person shares this letter? Then what?" she asked.

"We eliminate that possibility by only having one at a time available to play."

She didn't know why, but she immediately reached for the initials of her best friends and her own. She retrieved her letters and placed them into Jock's hands.

"Whether you know it or not, you chose some heavy hitters. Yes ma'am... shit is about to get nasty. Pour yourself some wine and relax. I'll be back in a few."

Chassidy held her composure up until he walked away and then she lost it.

"Chass are you crazy? You haven't had sex with one guy in a hundred years. What makes you think you can handle six at one time?!" she asked herself.

She filled her wine glass to the brim and took it to the head. She finished that glass and poured herself another one. The walls were covered with photos of people participating in orgies. The people in the photos looked happy, free and full of passion.

"Which picture holds your attention the most?"

"Jock you're so nosy. First, my favorite number and now this..."

She spun around to see six butt naked individuals staring at her. What really made her mouth drop to the floor was two of

PLEASURE PALACE

the individuals were women. Women were going to make love to her. She wasn't quite sure if she was ready for her first girl on girl experience.

"Chassidy meet your alphabet lovers..."

Jock stepped next to Chassidy and fondled her ass.

"I know he looks like the actor Mehcad Brooks, but he's not...this is Blake."

Blake was bald, tall and milk chocolate. His lips were full and the deep laugh lines around his mouth were calling her tongue. She definitely wanted a piece of him.

"Standing next to him is Cameron, also known as The Plumber. I'll leave that to your imagination as to how he acquired that name. And this over here is the beautiful Xaria. She can eat pussy better than all of us... you'll see."

Chassidy swallowed so hard it hurt. She was starting to show her nervousness again, which was the total opposite of what she was trying to do. She didn't want them

Page 172

to think that she was scary or weak, but she was having a hard time showing otherwise.

"Over here is Kaleb, but the ladies nicknamed him The Energizer Bunny. He's made several women tap out or wave the white flag because of his endurance. He's my idle."

Everyone but Chassidy laughed. She wasn't amused. She was starting to worry about her insides. It sounded like these people were going to rip her apart.

"Last but not least, this is Amarie. She's here to make us all bust! Hey Chass, you can't have all of the fun, now can she friends?"

"Not if I have anything to say about it?" said Amarie.

Blake closed the distance between them and stroked her hair behind her ear.

"You seem afraid, but you have sex on your mind. I can see it in your eyes.

"Oh really?"

His arms softly snaked around her waist.

"Yes. They're saying fuck me tough...fuck me rough...fuck me long... long…time..."

Shock flashed across her face. He brought her into his arms and laid her on the bed.

"I like your lips. They look delicious."

The gaze he held said *I picked you to fuck*, even though it was the other way around.

He nuzzled his mouth to hers. Slowly brushing his lips back and forth across hers, he tried to open her legs. She refused.

"Relax. We're horny...you're horny...let us give you what you need."

Chassidy took a deep breath and relaxed her thighs. She flinched when she felt two more pairs of hands on her...and then a mouth. A small warm mouth trapped her nipples. She opened her mouth to gasp only to be greeted with an erratic tongue. Her eyes shot open to find that it was Xaria's tongue down her throat and Amarie's lips holding her breasts hostage. It felt too good to contest, so she opened her legs wider and kissed Xaria deeper.

"Yes baby, let me in. Let us please you."

Blake massaged her clit in a slow rhythm. His tongue trailed the length of her thigh making her jerk.

"Move over, it's our turn." said Kaleb.

He poured wine into Chassidy's mouth and drizzled it down her body and drenched her pussy with it. Cameron's and Jock's mouths were on her in an instant. Cameron's lips were like candied flames against her skin. His kisses sizzled, burned and blazed, setting her on fire. Jock licked every inch of her skin. Her body felt alive and sexy. Cameron...he gently caressed her hot spots with his sweltering tongue. They touched every single part of her with every single part of them.

"Open your eyes Chassidy and watch me make you lose your mind."

Xaria grabbed the honey on the side of the bed and coated Chassidy's pussy with it. Her tongue began to work Chassidy's body furiously. It was as if she was hungry and could no longer tame her lust and desire. She inserted two fingers and sucked her clit like a lemon.

"Ooh you're tight as hell!"

Chassidy could feel her climax nearing. She locked her ankles around her pleaser's neck and gyrated against her tongue. Her moans were high and overlapped each other.

"Ah shit Xaria, here she comes! This has to be a personal best for you." yelled Jock.

"Oooh right there, don't stop...don't stop... I'm cuming!"

Xaria came up like she'd been washing her face. From her nose to her chin was glistening with Chassidy's juices. Amarie licked Xaria's face clean before pushing her onto the floor and burying her face between her legs.

"You don't have time to catch your breath. Turnover and arch your back for me baby."

She obeyed, and he poured wine on the nape of her neck and watched it run down her back; giving her asshole a little flavor. He finger fucked her pussy and tongue fucked her asshole simultaneously. Cameron brought sounds out of her that she didn't know she possessed. There was another pair of lips on hers... again. Kissing, sucking, and wrestling with her tongue...again.

"Are you ready for some double fun baby?" Kaleb asked as he lay next to her.

Cameron answered for her. He pulled her off the bed, which allowed Kaleb to scoot to the edge.

"Climb on top."
Kaleb grabbed her hand and laid back. She straddled him and sat down on his pole carefully. He pulled her into him and kissed her hard and slowly. *Jesus he is a hell of a kisser*. She was so caught up that she didn't pay attention to Cameron rubbing her asshole with his dick...until he tried to enter. She broke her lip-lock and looked back.

"I've never... I've never done that before." she confessed.

"I won't hurt you. Just take deep breaths when you feel pressure. I'll be gentle." Cameron assured her.

Kaleb licked her lips and she was back distracted by his hungry kisses. She felt Kaleb spread her ass cheeks and Cameron open her hole. One thrust... two... three... four... he was in. Once Cameron picked up his rhythm, Kaleb followed suit and pumped in and out of her.

"Come on baby, bounce on this dick. Pop that ass. I know you can."

His words brought the beast out of her. She bounced, clapped and popped her ass like she worked at the strip club. "Oooh fuck! Keep doing that shit! You're going to make me nut all up in this ass." Cameron moaned.

She bucked her ass against him hard and fast.

"Mmmm, you should see your face Kaleb, the energizer bunny huh? You're about to cum aren't you?"

"You have that Ill-na-na mama. Your pussy is too tight and wet." he replied.

PLEASURE PALACE

Xaria let out a long moan and a bunch of curse words.

"Good job Amarie. Now it's my turn."

Jock snatched Amarie up by the hair and smashed her face in his crotch. Without hesitation Amarie took all of him in her mouth. He swore back to back.

"Shit I'm about to cum again."

Kaleb grabbed Chassidy by the hips and bounced her up and down so hard that her breasts smacked him on the chin.

All three of them came one by one. Chassidy collapsed onto Kaleb when Cameron pulled out of her. Cameron fell to his knees and smacked her on the ass.

"You have some good shit girl, damn."

She looked up at Blake and saw the desire in his eyes, but she didn't know if she had enough energy or another orgasm to give.

"I know what you're thinking, and I *will* make you cum again." said Blake.

He crawled his way to her and pulled her off of Kaleb. He feathered kisses from her waist to her toes. His wet boiling kisses put life back into her clit. It was starting to pulsate. His mouth...it housed a powerful animal and it was ready to take her alive. He sat his cock on her stomach and stared at her. She gasped and salivated at his divine length.

"Lick the head until I tell you to stop."

She sat up and did what she was told. Chassidy ran the tip of his dick down her tongue over and over, savoring his salty pre-cum.

"That's enough."

He repeatedly thumped her wet tender spot with the head of his cock. Without warning he rammed into her with force. She yelled and he covered her mouth with his. He pushed even harder the second time and filled her center with his throbbing member. She trembled and moaned against the hardness of him.

"Open your eyes Chassidy. Let's watch each other enjoy one another."

PLEASURE PALACE

Her pussy welcomed him. She fought to keep her eyes open against the pleasure she was feeling.

He was inside of her like it was the one place in this world that he was meant to be. They moved their hips in unison. Grinding, winding, and bumping into each other like maniacs. Xaria came over and tongued them down, setting both of their bodies aflame with unbridled desire. He switched speeds and sent her into a moaning frenzy.

"Yea get her Blake! Make her leak!" screamed Xaria.

Jock smacked the wall again and again with force as he shot his seed down Amarie's throat.

"Cameron go over there and give Amarie a reason to scream. I'll give Kaleb one." Xaria suggested.

It felt like she was going to pass out. The orgasm took over her with so much power that she dug her nails into his back and screamed against his throat. Pressing his mouth to hers, their moans became one vibration. The two of them exchanged sexy noises and rugged breaths. She loved it.

"Fuck Chassidy! Fuck! Shit!" Blake shot into her quivering and shaking violently.

They lay in each other's arms for a few moments fighting to get air into their lungs. She managed to find the strength to push Blake to the side. Even though she was utterly exhausted, she was still very much turned on. Jock was hitting Xaria from behind while she sucked Kaleb's dick. Cameron was on the other side of the room blowing Amarie's back out. Chassidy went around the room kissing, licking, biting and rubbing on them all. She slid under Amarie and began to eat her out. She was a rookie at this, but at this point it didn't matter. They were all high off sex and were going to fuck each other into the next day. Blake joined in on the fun and slurped on Chassidy's pussy like he was dying of thirst. He knew just what to do with a juicy center. Sounds of passion and satisfaction took over the room as all of them reached the highest peak of ecstasy while collapsing and tangling up in each other. They were trying to hang on to the most dynamic orgasms they'd ever had.

PART IV:
MORE...SO MUCH MORE

Locking **lips**

Locking **hips**

Taking suicide dips

Into a sea of ecstasy

You left my **soul** messy

I **climaxed** all over my core

You're the cause and the **cure**

Heal me with your **lustful kisses**

Our bodies **glisten** where we licked it

Desire is our tool

And we write sentences of our **sins**

From our chins to our shins

You have **orgasms** inside of you that I want

and I will not be denied

I came to claim that **victory**

PLEASURE PALACE

Standing **aroused** and bare

I came to win

CHAPTER XVIII

Meanwhile in the Cocktale Bar...

Savior had her up against the wall in a Kama sutra position called The Clasp. Bren's legs were firmly wrapped around his waist, leaving him no other option but to enter her. His muscular arms supported her ass as he teasingly penetrated her sanctum deeply. Exchanging sloppy kisses, they did an intense reggae dance winding and grinding fluently in each other's arms. There were no words spoken this time as sexual sound effects filled the air. An addict for her scream, he bobbed in and out of her ocean like he was drowning. Bren squeezed her thighs and pussy muscles tighter and tighter, making him ready to let go and sink. He carried her to the bed and kissed her with authority… biting, pulling, and licking all of her sweet spots like they belonged to him. She was trying to stop her nut from raging out, but he banged her like an angry drummer, hitting her g-spot furiously. She'd dug her nails so deep into his back that she was sure she'd broken through his skin. He felt no pain, just pleasure, because he worked her ass out nice and good. She let his massive dick take her mind, body and soul away to a place of ecstasy she never ever wanted to part with. They were zoned out.

Pounding...screaming...clawing...swearing non-stop. They finally gave in and climaxed themselves into jerking fits.

"I know this is a sex club, but I think we just made love."

He rolled onto his side and pulled her close to him.

"I think you're right." she responded.

"I didn't think I would retire this early. I said to myself that the day I make love to a woman would be the day that I give up the gigolo lifestyle and try my hand at being a one woman man. Shit. I just knew that was going to happen in my forties, not in my thirties."

"Things happen for a reason. Maybe I was just what the doctor ordered to get you to put down your player cards." She said while attempting to catch a yawn escaping her mouth.

"I see it's someone's bedtime. If you need to suck on my cock to fall asleep, you are more than welcome to do so."

"Please, I'm sore as hell, so on that note, help me wrap this towel back on so I can go home and soak in a bath for the next two weeks. I'm betting that's how long it's going to take for me to properly heal from the beating you've put on my coochie."

"Coochie? What are we in fifth grade again? And for your information, you aren't the only one who's achy around here. You squeezed your pussy so tight, it's like you had my dick in a headlock."

Bren laughed.

"Well my kitty wasn't given the name Vise Grip for nothing. You can thank all of the kegel exercises done in hot vinegar baths for my pussy being so tight."

Her body felt so heavy like she had swallowed a ton of bricks.

"Carry me to my clothes please?"

He scooped her in his arms and carried her into the Cocktale lounge. Red smiled and winked at the lovers when they walked past.

"This is a first, Savior. You usually leave them in the back crying and bleeding. She must have been good." said Red.

Bren threw a wink back at Red and they both giggled like school girls.

Inside The ER...

They moved the action from the gurney to a small stool. She wanted to fuck in a position called The Waterfall and he was game. Aleric sat down gently with her straddling him. Jelly leaned into a back bend, resting her head on a pillow on the floor. She had proved that flexibility wasn't an issue for her and that she could handle his foot long dick, so she flexed her body effortlessly. After adjusting and getting comfortable, he immediately attacked her nipples with his thumbs and stroked in and out of her hard and deep. She held him by the elbows and flexed her pussy in his lap. His hands abused her breasts as he squeezed

and pinched her nipples and sent jolts of
pain mixed with pleasure through her body.
She felt so warm and wet around his cock. .
His pulse was misbehaving. He wanted to
stay inside of her until neither one of them
could take it any longer

Her long drawn out moans drove him
over the brink and the beast in him wasn't
going to go over the edge alone. She was
coming with him. Aleric released her breasts
and grabbed her by the arms and went into
overdrive.

"Ahhhh...Aleric baby slow... slow
down...I can't take it."

"Too bad, because I'm in control
now. I'm about to make this pussy cry me a
river."

He threw his head back and grunted
with each thrust. If it meant throwing his
back out to get her to beg him to stop, then
so be it. She tried to sit up, but his grip was
too strong. She could only lift her head up to
look at him. His face wore a look of pain
and his bottom lip was losing its color from
being bitten down on. She lost her focus
when she felt her pussy convulsing around

him. She was cuming... and quick. She dug into his elbows as her body began to jerk sporadically. His grunt became deeper...quicker...drilling into her with everything he had left. They yelled obscenities simultaneously before embracing each other like long lost loves. Still inside of her, Aleric slid from the stool onto the floor light headed and breathless from the night's festivities.

"I must say Miss Jelly; you sure are a good time."

"I must say the same for you Mister Aleric. You tore me up with that monster between your legs, but I took it like a big girl up until the end."

"Yea in that position I think I touched your heart with my big man King." he said.

"I think you did too, and you named him King?"

"Yep, that's been his name since high school. So what's your schedule like? How often do you work here?"

"Why? You plan on coming back to see me?"

He ran two fingers up and down her vagina and nodded his head yes.

"I'm here Thursdays, Fridays, and Saturdays."

"What do you do you Sunday through Wednesday?" he asked.

"I'm a graphic designer. I make websites, book covers, among other things for artists to business owners."

"Mmm mmm mmm! A business woman who's a bonafide freak! Can you cook?"

"Like I'm from the south." she replied.

"Whelp that's all I needed to know. What's your ring finger size?"

"Boy stop playing! You know you're not the settling down type. Most people who come in here either come with their significant other or live in here because they enjoy getting their needs met without being weighed down by the 'C' word."

He frowned.

"The 'C' word?"

"Commitment."

"Oh okay, I got you. Well how about you see me out, and we can switch numbers to make plans and discuss this under the sheets another time."

"Okay then, let's go."

He grabbed her by the waist and pulled her back down to the floor.

"Since it could be days... maybe even weeks before we see each other again, can you give King a big sloppy see you later kiss?"

Without a word she ran her tongue down his chest all the way to his shaft and took him into her mouth. She showered King with several kisses and licks before sending him on his way.

Over in the Sticky Kitty...

Kara and Elation had kicked off a hot and steamy game of alphabet sex. The object of the game was to use your tongue to spell a word beginning with each letter of the alphabet. The longer the word, the better. Whoever came first, lost. Kara had never performed oral sex in the sixty-nine position. She'd always been afraid she would bite some poor dude's dick off if she came too hard. With Elation it was different. She made it seem like eating pussy was an art to be practiced and mastered. Kara had just finished spelling out chocolate when Elation yelled out the next word.

"Delegation!"

Elation's tongue pressed firmly against Kara's clit for every line and loop. After spelling the word she gave the clitoris a little suck.

"Aye, that's cheating!"

"No it's not. That was a period. We can't forget punctuation, now can we?"

"Okay, you play dirty. The next word is elusive."

"I thought we were already playing dirty."

She smacked Kara's ass making it wobble along her face. They made it all of the way to the letter Q before clits swelled and moans escaped. Kara sucked Elation nice and hard before shouting out the next word.

"Quantity!"

They were starting to feel it. Their tongues moved swifter, harder, and driving one another insane while pressing down with each curve of each letter. Kara was bouncing on her lover's face while her lover was thrusting into hers. The heat and the tension had become unbearable; it wasn't long before one of them broke.

"Fuck this shit, I'm about to make you cum all over my face."

Elation plunged two fingers inside of Kara in search of her g-spot. Once located, she wasted no time working her tongue and probing fingers in unison to draw out cries of unrestrained passion.

Kara rode Elation's face like a professional jockey. With every ass smack she'd yell out *yes* and circle her nipples with her tongue. Elation's aggressive behavior brought out a side in Kara that Jeremy hadn't even seen. She shivered when her pleaser's mouth became a vacuum. She sucked on Kara like she'd been without an ounce of liquid for days, and she was dying to quench her thirst.

"Mmm Elation. You are so good. You are so damn good."

The more she moaned the harder Elation sucked. Her tongue was like an express train to the land of ecstasy that drove Kara to pure unapologetic satisfaction. She screamed and splashed right into Elation's mouth.

"Gotdamn! You are fucking amazing! Whew!"

"Thank you...thank you very much. Come here and taste yourself."

Kara was starting to dig kissing a woman. It was completely different from kissing a man. The lips are softer and sweeter.

"I think I know what I'm going to give my fiancé for his birthday." said Kara.

"And what's that?"

"A threesome. Are you interested?"

"How do you know I'm not a lesbian?" questioned Elation.

"Well if that's the case, you can just fuck me and I'll fuck him." Kara replied.

Elation laughed.

"No, I'm just messing with you. I'm bi-sexual, and if y'all talking good money I'll be there."

"Good, now let me give this pretty kitty a kiss until we meet again."

Elation put her legs above her head.

"Go ahead baby. Do the damn thing." Kara's inner lesbian wasn't trying to go back into hiding. She wanted to play some more. Kara was freaky, but never this freaky and her new found sexual freedom… she owed it all to Elation. She couldn't wait to see the look on Jeremy's face when she presented him with the idea of being pleased by his future wife and another woman. She really couldn't wait to see the look on Bren's face when she told the whole crew. Kara parted Elation's pussy lips and let her tongue lead the hunt for a final orgasm.

Back in the Suction Room…

Jeremy had Dior upside down in a standing sixty-nine position eating her out while she sucked him off.

"Let's go to the bed, I want to try something I found online the other day." She giggled against his shaft as he carried her to the bed.

"Lay back and spread your legs."

She crouched between his legs and began sucking him like there was no tomorrow.

"Not that I'm complaining, but what's so different about this? This is the same..."

Without removing her mouth from his cock, she quickly shifted her body over to his left side. Kneeling next to his left hip, she pushes him further into her mouth. Just when he was starting to wind his hips, she moved from that side position and straddled his chest. She clapped her ass in his face encouraging him to spank her. Not a selfish lover, Jeremy gave her some loving in return while she deep throated him. Dior lifted her leg and worked him from his right side. She sucked his dick clockwise with each angle providing different sensations. The gurgling sounds she made guided the nut right out of him. He plowed into her mouth with so much force he could've knocked her tonsils down her throat.

"Damn!"

He released his warm seed, shaking in between curse words and ass smacks.

"Damn baby, I'm going to have bruises on my ass after you get done beating it."

She wiped the corners of her mouth and laid her head on his chest.

"This is between me and you; you suck dick way better than my girl... and I mean way better."

"Well if you ever want me to give her some private lessons in the art of dick sucking, you know where to find me."

"Can I have that in writing?"

Jeremy and Dior lay in each other's arms teasing one another about their love faces and sounds. The two couldn't decide whether to keep the video or get rid of it. They ultimately decided to burn it after Jeremy's fingers found their way inside of her.

PLEASURE PALACE

The competition continues...

Eden wasn't too fond of Xavier having his way with her, so she planned to show him who was boss before he left the club. She led him by the hand to a back room with nothing but a mat with a small bed in the middle of it.

"We're all alone now. What are you going to do to me?" she asked walking backwards onto the mat.

He slid on a condom and rushed her. He scooped her into his arms and tongued her down and stole her breath.

"Have you ever fucked in the suspended scissors position?" he asked in a whisper.

"Yes, but I wouldn't mind doing it again with you." she said.

"With your small build, are you sure you have the strength to hold yourself up? You do know that this position requires some serious muscle?"

She looked back at him and smiled.

"If you're too weak to perform this position it's okay to say so. I mean, you did just fuck three women."

Eden should've known by now that Xavier didn't like to be challenged.

"Yea, but who came first? Me or y'all? Now lie down on the edge of the bed. You know what to do."

And indeed she did.

He lifted her up by the waist and stepped over her left leg. Holding her other leg, he penetrated her and instantly picked up where they left off.

"Mmm hmm, all I hear are moans. What happened to all that shit talking you was doing? Let me hear you talk that shit now."

Her pussy made a squishy sound as he rammed in and out of her. He'd learned a long time ago that certain positions like this one allowed for deep penetration which brought on explosive orgasms.

"Is this dick good? Huh? Tell me that my shit is good. Tell me that you like this dick."

Page 200

PLEASURE PALACE

"Yes, yes, yes! This is the best dick I've ever had! I love this dick! I love it!"

That was all he needed to hear before he kicked into high speed to bring them both to the Promised Land.

"Oh shit! Shit! Shit! Shit!"

He fell to his knees while kissing and lingering inside of her.

"Xavier, I think I'm going to like seeing you for an entire month."

"The feeling is mutual. You better believe I'm going to take advantage of you every single day for thirty days straight."

She ran her tongue along her top lip and gave his balls a jiggle.

"For thirty days straight? I cannot wait to be fucked."

Down in Orgy Central...

Jock's scissors lost to Kaleb's rock, so he had to sit out for the last activity: the oral train. Chassidy, Blake, Cameron, Xaria, Amarie and Kaleb all lay down on their sides to form a human circle. Positioned male to female, they were to give oral pleasure to the person in front of them. They all went to town: sucking and slurping...fingering and licking...pulling on clits and dicks... just full-out mouth fucking one another. Chassidy was in heaven. She had never felt so good about being so nasty in her life, and this newfound sexual freedom was quickly becoming addictive.

Chassidy was sucking Blake's dick so good he stopped eating Amarie's pussy just to tell her so. She couldn't respond because Cameron was eating the shit out her with his massive mouth. She was trying not to bite Blake's dick off, but her leg was trembling and her eyes kept rolling to the back of her head. She felt herself losing control so she snatched his penis out of her mouth and braced herself for another amazing orgasm. Her thighs tightened around his head as he zig-zagged his tongue roughly back and forth across her clit.

"Oohhh Myyy Goddd! Oooo!"

Chassidy splashed her warm juices right onto Cameron's face. She quickly caught her second wind and finished Blake off. One by one they made each other climax. Soon they were lying entangled and gasping for air.

"If I could, I'd marry all of you motherfuckas. You guys were great!" Chassidy exclaimed.

They all laughed.

"Come back to see us any time and we'll hook you up again, won't we pleasers?" Xaria said.

Chassidy smiled when she heard everyone agree.

"Look don't talk that shit and don't be available when I want you, because then I'll be pissed! Now who's going to help me up?"

Chassidy threw up her hands when no one responded.

"Are y'all serious? Do we have to do rock, paper, scissors again to see who's going to help me get off this damn floor?" she asked.

All five of them raised their hands in the air.

Chassidy threw her head back.

"Well shit."

PLEASURE PALACE

She shook her head and lifted her
hands in the air like the rest of them.

CHAPTER XIX

The Sun was coming up when Kara stepped outside. She was high off sex and trying her best to stand up straight. She did her best to remove the stupid little grin from her face before Jeremy saw her. She felt great and guilty at the same time. Elation did things to her body that Jeremy hadn't. Hell, she unleashed a side of herself with Elation that Jeremy has never seen. A thought hit her like a baseball to the face. *What if Jeremy got so turned out that he won't be satisfied with me anymore*? The door swung open startling her out of her thoughts.

"Jeremy?"

Kara turned around to see two big brown beady eyes staring at her.

"Oh it's you Xavier. Have you seen Jeremy?"

"Nah I haven't seen him. Your ass look drunk. How much wine did you have?" he asked.

"Too damn much. What about you brother? You look like you just finished running a triathlon."

"My destination was the Sexercise Room, remember? What the hell do you think happened in there? I'm tired as shit."

"Yea you're tired alright. I knew that The Pleasure Palace would be too much for you."

Xavier looked over his shoulder and frowned.

"Bren shut your ass up! You just got out here and you're talking shit! And what's wrong with your legs? Dude beat the pussy up like that? You okay? Need a wheelchair?"

Kara and Xavier burst into laughter while making fun of their friend's bow legs.

"Fuck both of you. He had a damn python between his legs, but big girls don't cry. I took it all like a champ! Chassidy needs to hurry up so she can bring the car up to the curb. My legs are shot!"

"Who got shot?" asked Aleric.

"Leric what's up dude? Why are you rolling your shoulders and twisting from side to side?" Bren asked curiously.

"Because ole girl turned into a cow girl in zero point two seconds. Man she rode my ass to death in all kinds of ways! What about y'all?"

"As you can see, some dude has knocked out the little lining Bren had left in her pussy. She's walking around waddling like a penguin."

"Shut the hell up Xay!"

"And I won a sex race. I'm a beast, but I told y'all that all ready."

Aleric shook Xavier's hand.

"No doubt. That's what's up. How did it go for you Kara?"

"Uh, I'd rather not say Leric."

"Hell no Kara! You know what happened with us. We want to know who rocked your boat and how they did it!" yelled Bren.

"Yea baby, who rocked your boat and how did they do it?"

A look of fear flashed across Kara's face when she saw her fiancé approaching the group.

"Jeremy! Hey baby. Did you have a good time in there?" Kara asked without answering the question.

"You first." Jeremy said folding his arms.

Aleric, Bren and Xavier gawked at the couple like they were watching a disaster in progress. Kara cleared her throat.

"To be honest honey, I did. Surprisingly I had a wonderful time."

"A wonderful time huh? So he was that good?" questioned Jeremy.

"She baby, it was a she, and she was amazing...for real for real."

"Kara, oh my God you had your first lesbian experience? Girl I want details!" shouted Bren.

"I did too. Actually I was pleased by two women and four men." Chassidy said tip toeing to the crowd.

"Damn they have you walking funny too! These dudes must use penis pumps or something!"

"SHUT UP XAY!" everyone yelled.

"But anywho... a chick? You gave my goodies away to a chick? Did she lick it better than me?"

Kara lowered her head to the ground answering Jeremy's question in silence.

"Humph, I guess I need to brush up on my skills, huh?"

"Would you like to have a threesome with her for your birthday?!" Kara blurted out.

Everyone's mouths dropped open, including hers.

"How about a foursome? Because the chick I was with tonight gave me some head that was out of this world and she volunteered to teach you a few tricks." he replied.

"Damn baby just put my business out like that! I give bomb head!"

"Yes baby you do, but she gives it better."

The whole crew gasped and turned away simultaneously.

"We'll see about that buddy. As soon as we recuperate it's on!" Kara said matter-of-factly.

"Wait a minute! Wait a damn minute! You both aren't mad at each other? So you're telling me that neither of you are pissed at the other for enjoying fucking and being fucked by other people tonight?" Bren asked.

Kara and Jeremy both shook their heads no.

"This is some ole bullshit! No one's love is that strong!"

"Bren I'm going to punch you in the face if you don't stop hating! They love each other damnit, and if you or anybody else can't handle that, then maybe you need to remove yourselves from their world." said Chassidy.

"I'm sorry, you're right. Okay fine! I'm a tad bit jealous okay! We always said that I'd be the first to get married. It was always supposed to be me. Fuck… y'all I'm sorry. You know I love you two."

Bren walked over and gave the couple a huge hug.

Chassidy was about to cry. Xavier shook his head and Aleric rolled his eyes at all of them.

"So it's really happening. We're still getting married?" asked Jeremy.

Kara stood on her tip toes and kissed him on the cheek.

"Of course we are honey, we're in this forever."

"I'll get the car." said Aleric.

"Yea Chass go get the car. I can't walk all the way over there. I feel like my vagina is hanging on by a thread."

"Ugh Bren, too much information!" said Jeremy.

"Well hell it's the truth. I honestly think dude rearranged my insides. I'm pretty sure nothing is where it's supposed to be." said Bren.

Everyone laughed except Xavier.

"What's wrong with you Xay? I just knew you would have a joke to crack on her." said Kara.

"Nothing, I'm good. I just don't see why someone would brag about painful sex that's all." he said.

"No doubt it was painful, but chile let me tell you, I never came so much and so hard in my life! I'll heal all up and come back for some more. I'm not lying!"

"Man I don't want to hear that shit. Bye!" said Xavier as he hopped inside of Aleric's car.

"Uh oh, someone's jealous isn't he?" Bren taunted.

"I say this on behalf of myself, my future wife and our buddies Chassidy and Aleric...we will all be glad when you and Xavier stop playing these juvenile ass games and fuck each other's brains out. All of this bickering y'all do is getting old and annoying. Why don't y'all just bust a few nuts and call it truce?" said Jeremy while helping Bren into the car.

"When he's ready for me, he knows where to find me. Be sure to tell him that."

Jeremy shook his head and slammed the car door. He made a mental note to add those two to his bedtime prayers. He walked over to Kara's window and leaned in for a kiss.

"See you at home baby. We're going to take a nice long shower and sleep the day away." he said.

"Sounds good to me. I can't wait."

He stepped away from the car and watched it disappear down the road.

"Yea you say you still want to get married next weekend, but we'll see if your mind stays the same. This is going to be an interesting seven days, I'll tell you that much."

"Yo Jeremy get your ass in the car! We're ready to go!" yelled Xavier.

Jeremy climbed into the car and lied down in the back seat.

"Dude what's wrong with you? And what were you talking about out there?" asked Aleric.

"Nothing. Just drive man."

"Okay well I'm telling my story first. Man this chick was bad! Her name is Jelly and she was..."

Jeremy's attention went to his vibrating phone. It was a message from Kara.

"We need to talk as soon as we get home." it read.

He lip read it and instantly tossed his phone on the floor.

PLEASURE PALACE

"Aw Shit."

<u>CHAPTER XX</u>

He woke up Monday morning refreshed. After Jeremy told them about the text he received from Kara in the car, he just knew that his plan had worked. At first he thought it fell through when Kara dropped that bomb and asked Jeremy if he wanted to have a threesome for his birthday. He knew that she was fronting like what happened inside that club didn't bother her. Yep he was in a good place. He absolutely loved getting his way. He opened an ice cold beer and threw it back with a sinister smile on his face. Meek Mill's voice blasted through the room, snapping him out of thought.

"Jesus Christ, Meek, let me put your ass on vibrate. Hello? What's up Jeremy?"

"Aye man I'm just touching bases to let you know that the wedding is still on. I thought we were about to break up when y'all dropped me off yesterday, but she apologized instead."

He took deep breaths to hide the anger and disappointment in his voice.

"Apologized for what?"

"For liking her lesbian experience and for asking me if I wanted a threesome in front of everyone. I told her that it was cool, and I wasn't going anywhere. We talked a bit more about it and decided that this was a test we proudly passed."

He said about twenty 'fucks' under his breath before responding.

"Hello? Are you still there?" asked Jeremy.

"Yea I'm still here."

"Yea so make sure the tuxes are ready for pick up on Thursday and everything else I left you in charge of. I picked you as my first best man for a reason. I'll talk to you later, one."

"One."

He hung up the phone furious. Pacing the floor like a mad man, he threw the beer bottle against the wall.

"Fuck! Fuck! Fuck! This is some straight bullshit!"

How could this happen? Once again Jeremy was going to come out on top.

"Okay, y'all still want to get married? Fine. Watch it be the most disastrous day of y'all lives. I'm tired of this fucker getting his hands on every gotdamn thing that I want! I'm sick of it! And that uppity bitch Kara...who the fuck is she to turn me down? I've played nice for too damn long. I'm done being the phony supportive best friend. Shit is about to get real! They think that they know me, BUT THEY DON'T KNOW SHIT!"

He printed the list of all the duties he was responsible for in regards to the wedding and headed out the door. The wedding was only a few days away, so if he was going to wreck shit, he had to wreck it now. His first stop was Mr. Barry's tuxedo shop over on North Avenue and Narragansett. Mr. Barry was old and senile; he wasn't going to suspect a thing.

"Hey Mr. Barry, how are you doing old man?"

"Hey there young blood. I'm good and yourself?"

"Oh I'm good Mr. Barry. I just came to make sure our tuxes will be ready for pick up Thursday afternoon. You know the wedding is Saturday."

"Boy I may have lost the majority of my eyesight and a lot of my hearing, but I still have my mind. Of course I know the wedding is this weekend. Let me go grab them for you."

"No sweat Mr. Barry. I'm just here to make sure everything is right for my best buddy's wedding."

Mr. Barry came back with three black garment covers. He unzipped the bags and showed the tailor-made suits.

"Here you go. Everything was adjusted immediately after the last fitting. Snug but comfortable, I believe was Mr. Jeremy's request."

"Great, but where are the vests? I'd like to see those too if you don't mind."

"Oh yes, the vests! I had to press those out. Be right back."

He waited until the old man was out of sight before he reached inside of his pocket and pulled out a box cutter. He slashed the groom's suit up to the point where he would need more than a needle and thread to repair the damage. He would need an entire new tuxedo. He hurried and zipped up all three covers before Mr. Barry came back.

"Those vests are fly Mr. Barry! Jeremy is going to be pleased."

"I hope so. I've worked on these things for weeks! Let me just put these inside with the suits."

"NO! No need for that. Besides, they look like they can be pressed a bit more. The tuxedos look perfect as they are, so I wouldn't suggest messing them up by stuffing the vests inside. Keep these zipped tight and put the vests under some plastic."

"Are you sure?" asked Mr. Barry.

"Yes, believe me; Jeremy would want it this way."

"Well okay if you insist. See you Thursday."

"See you Thursday Mr. Barry."

He shook the old man's hand and left. He took out the list and marked a check next to pick up tuxedos.

"Next stop is the Allen Edmonds men's store for the shoes, and then off to cancel the barbershop and spa appointments. Oh yea I can't forget to cancel the horse and carriage. That was my 'pretend that I'm happy for the both of you' wedding gift anyway."

He dedicated his entire day to slowly ruining his best friend's wedding. He sat out front of the barbershop and shot Jeremy a text.

"Aye bro, everything is in place for your big day."

He literally laughed out loud when he read Jeremy's response.

"Thanks bro. Saturday can't come fast enough. Holler at you later." it read.

"No problem. You know that I have your back. If you need anything else, hit me up."

He hit send and tossed his phone into the passenger seat.

"That's something we can both agree on. Saturday can't come fast enough. I can't wait to see the look on you and Kara's faces."

He was finally in a better mood until his phone rang again.

"How may I help you?" he answered.

"I was just calling to see what was up? Were we good actors and actresses or what?"

"Yea you were Eden, but the plan fell through. Those idiots are still getting married."

"Damn, well I guess they were meant to be, huh?"

He looked at the phone with disgust.

"What the fuck ever. I have to go."

"Wait, are we still on for later?"

"Only if you make sure my second favorite joins us." he said.

"No problem baby. I'll make sure that she's there."

He shook his head and hung up.

"Damn she's a thirsty bitch."

CHAPTER XXI

Kara was running around like a chicken with its head cut off. She was on the phone all day with Jeremy making sure he didn't forget to pick up his attire for the wedding. The three glasses of Moscato did nothing to calm her nerves, and she was driving Chassidy and Bren crazy by making them repeatedly go over her wedding check list.

"I'm sorry y'all, but the wedding is in two days and I just have to make sure everything is taken care of. I want to eliminate as many mishaps and as much confusion as I can. We all know weddings never go exactly as planned, but dammit, mine will be as close to perfect as possible because well... well because I said so shit! Chass let's go over the list one more time."

"Lord have mercy Kara, again?!" Bren asked exasperatedly.

"Girl shut the hell up! Chassidy...read!"

PLEASURE PALACE

"Flowers, catering, band, wait staff, limos, dresses, shoes, accessories, hair, nails and spa appointments, the photographer, and the videographers are all set for Saturday."

"And the hotel rooms for our parents?"

"They will be able to check in on Friday after two o'clock." responded Chassidy.

"No bridesmaids and grooms have dropped out right?" asked Kara.

"Nope, everyone is still on board. Will you calm down now? Nothing is going to go wrong."

"Chile I'll calm down when the reverend says, 'I now pronounce you husband and wife'." said Kara.

"Please, you're going to loosen up at your bachelorette party on Friday night if I have anything to say about it." said Bren.

Kara looked back and forth at her maids of honor.

"Are y'all serious? A bachelorette party? The Pleasure Palace wasn't enough for you two?"

"I don't know about Chass, but it damn sure wasn't enough for me." said Bren.

"Kara it's tradition for the bride-to-be to have a party to celebrate her last and final night being a single woman. You know this." Chassidy stated.

"And besides, you think Xavier and Aleric didn't plan a bachelor party for Jeremy? Please! Knowing those two fools, they probably invited the broads from the club to join the party."

"Bren you know what I was hoping would happen that night?" Kara asked.

"No, what?"

"I was hoping that someway… somehow Xavier's dick found its way inside your pussy! I'm so ready for y'all to fuck I don't know what to do!" yelled Kara.

"We are ALL ready for y'all to hit the sheets. You know you want to." said Chassidy.

"It's not me, it's him. He's not ready for this jelly!"

She started popping her ass and Kara laughed.

PLEASURE PALACE

"Bren you are a damn fool. Who did you hire to shake their ass for me?"
"That's a surprise, my love. A surprise that you're going to be thanking me for in years to come, because you know I only fuck with the best. They are tall, handsome, and thick and they hang low. Be ready to be entertained ladies."

"Um Ms. Kara, you still haven't gotten into detail about what exactly happened in The Sticky Kitty room. Are you ever going to share?" asked Bren.

Kara rested the rim of her wine glass on her lip.

"Now Bren, what makes you think I will tell you anything after you set the entire Pleasure Palace scheme up based on me sharing with you, my best friend, my amazing intimate moments with my man? Oh no honey. First time, shame on you. Second time, shame on me, so I'm good."

Bren tried not to show the hurt in her face, so she quickly raised her glass and proposed a toast.

"I can respect that Kara. May you and Jeremy live happily ever after. To love and friendship."

Kara and Chassidy echoed Bren and clinked their glasses.

Jeremy stared at his tuxedo with his mouth to the floor. He did a double, triple, quadruple take at his sliced up clothing.

"Mr. Barry, what...in the hell...happened?"

"Jeremy I honestly don't know. Your tux was perfectly fine on Monday when, who was that, Aleric or Xavier came in to check on it. There is no way I can repair this by Saturday morning. We're going to have to get you a new tuxedo."

"It was Aleric and Mr. Barry my fiancé is going to have a heart attack if she sees this. Please, you have to do something."

Kara's ringtone sounded off as if she knew he was thinking about her.

"Hey baby what's up?"

"Hey honey, some crazy shit is going on."

"Yea, you're telling me." he said.

"The girls and I were leaving out the house to go shopping, when I looked over at my car and the tires are slashed. Not only that, but your barber Kevin drove down our street and saw us. He double parked in front of the house and got out of his car asking why you cancelled your appointment, and if we were still getting married?"

"What the fuck?"

"That's exactly what I said and that's not all. He said Aleric was the one who cancelled the appointment."

"Damn baby I didn't even pay attention to your car when I left out and why in the hell would Aleric do that? Hold on baby let me call you right back, it's Xay on my other line. Maybe he has heard from Aleric." said Jeremy.

"Hey Xay what's up my dude?"

"Aye man, I go up to the spa place to get a foot detox and the chick at the front desk that I occasionally bang tells me that our Saturday morning appointment has been cancelled. What's up with that?"

"I'm going to kill that motherfucka."

"Who?!" yelled Xavier.

"Aleric."

"You think Leric had something to do with this? Why would he cancel shit and not tell us?" asked Xavier.

"I don't know. All I know is someone slashed my baby's tires, my tuxedo looks like Edward Scissorhands and Freddie Kruger were playing tug-of-war with it. Our appointments at the barber shop were cancelled, and now you're telling me this. Aleric was the only one in charge of all of this shit. I've been texting him since this morning and he hasn't responded to any of my messages." said Jeremy.

"Yea, he hasn't hit me back either. I usually hear from him every day. This is so out of his character. Damn man what the fuck is going on?!"

"If he shows up tomorrow to the bachelor party, you better believe that fucker will answer for all of this shit or get dropped right where he stands, and that's on God."

CHAPTER XXII

"Baby you've been tense ever since yesterday. Please don't do anything that will have me meeting you in jail instead of at the altar."

"Kara I'm telling you now, when I see him it's a done deal. I'm beating ass first and asking questions last. You already know me." said Jeremy.

"And so does he. Do you think he's really going to show his face at the party? I'm pretty sure he's figured out that we know about everything he tried to sabotage. Don't you want to know why he did it?"

"Yea I do, and I'll find out after I smack the fuck out of him."

Kara threw her hands in the air in frustration. She knew her future husband like the back of her hand, and when he set his mind to do something, he was going to do it.

"Xavier just pulled up outside. I'll see you tomorrow…one o'clock on the dot my love."

He pulled her into his arms and gave her a few quick kisses.

"Okay have fun baby and don't kill Aleric please. At least find out why first. He's still your best friend. Promise me."

"Kara I love you, but I can't make that promise. Have a good time tonight, and I'll see you later."

Jeremy got into Xavier's truck and sunk into the passenger seat.

"You alright man? Still haven't heard from Aleric?"

"Nope."

"Man Jeremy I know you. Don't do anything crazy for two reasons: number one, you don't want to get locked up and miss your wedding and possibly lose the love of your life and number two, everything inside of my house is brand new. If you two bastards break anything, I will be hitting up y'all pockets." said Xavier.

"Just drive man. Nobody is going to tear your crib up. I'm good."

Kara couldn't enjoy her bachelorette party because she was too worried about what Jeremy was going to do when he saw Aleric. She sat on the stairs and watched all of her guests drink, dance, laugh, and mingle amongst each other. She was being a Debbie Downer at her own party and no one seemed to notice, at least that's what she thought.

"Kara, you've been sitting over here looking like a little girl who lost her puppy. Cheer up. Jeremy is going to be fine." Chassidy said as she sat next to her best friend.

"Chass, I don't know. He had that same look in his eyes that he had the night he beat that valet guy into a coma for stealing money out of my car." said Kara.

"Oh Lord, well that's not good. You think he's going to do that to Aleric?"

Kara looked her friend dead in the eyes.

"I don't think so. I know so."

Jeremy's mind had been racing all day. He thought knocking back a couple of shots would make him not want to smash Aleric's face in so bad, but he was wrong. The liquor made him feel worse.

PLEASURE PALACE

"Aye listen up fellas! We've drank, we've eaten, we've laughed and caught up on old times, but now it's time for the real fun. On the other side of this door are some of the baddest strippers in the Midwest! So fellas, without further ado, I'd like for you to say hello to Divine, Desire, Cherry and Paradise!"

Xavier opened the door to his bedroom and out walked four multi-colored bombshells. Caramel, Chocolate, Vanilla and Mocha skinned women with watermelon sized breasts and apple bottom asses strutted out to the middle of the floor.

"Ladies you see that gentleman over there with the serial killer look on his face? Yea that's the groom and he needs a little cheering up. Do you mind?" Xavier asked.

"Of course we don't. Let's go put a smile on his face ladies." said Cherry.

"Looks like I came just in time to see the action. Xay you should really keep your doors locked. Any maniac could've walked in here."

Aleric grabbed two vodka shots from a tray and threw them back before flashing

Jeremy a crooked smile. Jeremy removed
Paradise and Desire from his lap and walked
towards Aleric.

"Cool out Jeremy, don't do it!"

Aleric tried to step back, but Jeremy
knocked him back. He hit him with a
straight right. That was all it took for shit to
turn into an all-out brawl. Aleric got a few
good licks in but a left hook to the ribs threw
gasoline on an already raging fire within
Jeremy. He beat the shit out of Aleric. It
took Xavier and three other guys to pull
Jeremy off of Aleric. Blood was all over the
tables and floor. The furniture was turned
over along with broken liquor bottles.

"Fuck! Look what y'all did to my
crib!"

Jeremy broke free and kicked Aleric
in the stomach.

"Why did your bitch ass try to
sabotage my wedding?!" Jeremy shouted.

"Because you're a gotdamn thief!
You took her from me! You didn't even want
her!" yelled Aleric.

"Are you serious right now Aleric?"
Xavier asked in disbelief.

"All of this is over a girl? This motherfucka can't be serious!"

"You and Kara were supposed to break up after we left Pleasure Palace. That was the plan, but nooooo y'all had to still get married."

"So you were in on that shit with Bren? You two plotted and schemed on breaking up my engagement?" Jeremy wanted to know.

"Bren was a pawn. One day I overheard her talking about going to The Pleasure Palace, and I used that as my opportunity. The entire time everyone thought that Bren was working hard to end your very annoying relationship, but it wasn't her. It was me."

Aleric picked himself up from the floor and leaned against the wall.

"I paid Eden a visit and had her and her staff pretend like they didn't know me. I needed all of you to believe that it was my first time there, even though I'm a regular. I was hoping the club would rip you two apart and you would blame the entire thing on

Bren, but things don't always go as planned, so I went to plan B."

"Wait a minute. Wait a gotdamn minute! I won a free month of sleeping with the enemy? Was the victory faulty or did I really beat that pussy up? Aw hell naw! You know what Jeremy, fuck it! Whoop his bitch ass!" yelled Xavier.

"NO! Wait Jeremy. Wait." Aleric threw his hands out in pain.

"Beating me up is not going to beat the envy out of my heart. I've been jealous of you and Xay since high school. I felt like because I didn't possess your good looks or his chick magnet personality I had to work twice as hard to get to the same level. Having to bust my ass like that infuriated me over the years. I grew bitter and resentful."

"Your ass is tripping! Level? What fucking level Leric?!" Jeremy asked.

"Of acceptance. You know what? It doesn't matter anymore. You win Jeremy. You've always won. No matter what it was. Whether it was sports or women, you always managed to come out victorious. Well I'm done hating on the low. I'm done wishing I was you... hell the both of you. I'm going to take me and my cracked ribs to the emergency room. Good luck tomorrow."

The whole room was silent, shocked and appalled by Aleric's dark confessions and Jeremy's animalistic behavior. But it was Jeremy who broke the silence.

"We were boys. You could've talked to me. Shit didn't have to be like this. You're like a brother to me. I never thought of you as beneath me or even consciously tried to make you feel inferior. All of this shit that you're talking about is in your head. I didn't steal Kara from you. She chose me remember? But you are right about one thing: I didn't want her at the time. I thought we'd have a one night stand and go our separate ways. I never intended on falling in love with her. Hell, even though she chose me, you were always Kara's favorite between you and Xay... no offense Xay..."

"I'm totally offended. Especially after this shit!"

"She's going to be very hurt and disappointed, Aleric just like I am. How could you be so conniving? I thought we were tight enough to come to each other with anything good or bad. Guess I was wrong, huh?" said Jeremy with pain in his voice.

"Man this is pure craziness Aleric. You have me thinking that our entire brotherhood was fake. I'm feeling like this whole friendship was a crock of bullshit. I can't even say that I know who you truly are." said Xavier with tears in his eyes.

Softly sobbing, Aleric wiped his face with his shirt sleeve and pushed his words out.

"I sincerely apologize to the both of you. I really don't know what to say for myself." Too embarrassed to face them again, he spoke over his shoulder.

"Yo Jeremy, tell Kara that I'm sorry. Tell her that I said I'm so very very sorry...for everything, and that I hope she will forgive me someday."

He sucked in a shaky breath and closed the door behind him.

Jeremy shed a tear of his own, for he knew deep down that this would be the last

time that he would ever see his best friend
again.

CHAPTER XXIII

Aleric hid in the background of The Botanical Gardens watching an event come together that he tried to prevent. He didn't dare show his face after betraying and hurting his friends, so he made the wise decision to support them from afar. It was beautiful outside. The air was crisp and warm. Because of the fresh cut grass and flowers, a sweet fragrance lingered in the air. Everyone he saw had a smile on their face. The caterers raced to get the wedding cake out of the sun while dodging running children and a large number of guests. The wedding planner was also moving at high speed setting up extra chairs inside of the English Walled Garden where the ceremony would take place. A secluded area that radiates pure old fashion romance, the English Walled Garden represented Jeremy and Kara's love exactly. As a matter of fact, it was he who suggested the couple get married there to cater to Jeremy's love of the outdoors and Kara's love of flowers.

PLEASURE PALACE

He almost didn't make it. He was in so much pain from Jeremy using him as a punching bag that he could barely get out of bed. He had spent half the night at the emergency room getting diagnosed with two cracked ribs on his right side, a sprained right ankle and a black eye. He never imagined in a million years that he'd ever feel remorse for the way he'd felt over the years. It was kind of like Jeremy knocked guilt and shame into him, and he was feeling it deeply. The one thought that had been rotating in his mind since all of this happened was *I wish I could take it all back*. But he couldn't. Some things were just set in stone. Aleric's stomach flip-flopped when the guests started to take their seats inside of the garden.

He shut his eyes tightly and turned away when he saw Xavier step behind Jeremy. That was his spot, and it was hitting him harder than ever that last night was truly the end of their friendships. His breath caught in his throat when Chassidy emerged. God she was beautiful as always. Her hair was in a classy pin-up and her dark skin was radiant. He couldn't bear to think of how she must feel about him now. Even though he secretly yearned for Kara, Chassidy came in close second. She was definitely wife material, but he was so blinded by getting revenge that he missed out on a good woman.

Aleric laughed out loud and quickly covered his mouth. Bren was two-stepping down the aisle in a thigh-high dress and stilettos that lent her a few extra inches in height. She was beautiful, but Bren was an attention whore and today, even for her best friend's wedding, she had to stand out.

"Lord have mercy she looks amazing." He said when Kara appeared in the garden.

Everyone rose to their feet and looked in admiration as she walked down the aisle on the arm of her father. Her gown fit her snuggly in all the right places and her hair was pulled to the back in loose spiral curls.

Jeremy laid eyes on his bride and smiled the biggest smile Aleric had ever seen.

Kara's father kissed her on both cheeks and handed her off to Jeremy. The ceremony was short but emotional. They recited vows that they wrote for each other, used their individual flames to light one candle, and was pronounced Mr. and Mrs. Jeremy James. He clapped along with the guests when they erupted into applause. He watched the newly weds jog down the aisle through a cloud of bubbles being blown by the guests. Kisses, hugs and smiles were exchanged as the newlyweds led the way into a breathtaking canopied terrace for the reception. There was no way he could sneak inside and remain undetected, so he silently congratulated and said his goodbyes to his old friends.

"Aleric!"

"Fuck, who in the hell spotted me?" he said turning around slowly.

It was Jeremy, and he did not look thrilled to see him.

"What are you doing here? I thought I made it clear last night that we are done... for life."

"I know Jeremy. I just came to say goodbye."

"Dude you said that last night!" Jeremy stepped in closer.

"Jeremy stop!"

Kara was running towards them with fear in her eyes. Bren, Xavier and Chassidy followed closely behind.

"Fuck that Kara, he has to go!" yelled Jeremy.

"Yea get his ass up out of here! Setting people up and shit!" shouted Bren.

"Bren, I'm so..."

Bren hauled off and smacked the hell out of Aleric.

"Boy you can keep that sorry ass apology, because there is not one excuse for what you did and tried to do. I used to think Xavier was the problem, humph! Fooled the hell out of me!" she said.

"Okay, I deserved that Bren. I'm still very sorry." Aleric looked over at Kara and continued.

"But I didn't come here to cause trouble. I came here today to apologize to Kara face to face and to say goodbye to everyone."

"Everyone, can Aleric and I have a minute?" asked Kara.

"Hell no baby! I'm not leaving you with this creep! He might stab you or kidnap you. NO!" Jeremy said sternly.

"I'm not going to do anything to her."

"You damn right you're not, because I'm not leaving my wife alone with you."

"Jeremy honey, it's okay, you can see us from the tent."

"I'm sorry, but you have to forgive us for not believing anything that you say Aleric. I mean after all, you were secretly hating your two best friends while at the same time secretly lusting after one of your best friend's girlfriend. Did you stop there? Nope, you didn't..." Xavier stepped in front of Jeremy and continued.

"You went on to try and sabotage the love of two people who, in my opinion, worked hard and deserves to be where they are today. You plotted and schemed on how to destroy a union that you were falsely supporting and for what? Because she chose your best friend over you? You said that you don't have our physical good looks, but Aleric to tell you the truth, you don't look as good as we do on the inside either. We may be arrogant smart mouthed freaks, but when it comes to friendship and family, we practice love, loyalty and respect. You obviously feel differently, and that right there is what makes you ugly Aleric. You're worried about your face, but you need to worry about that ugly trifling ass spirit of yours instead."

Xavier shook his head and tapped Jeremy on the arm.

"I'm going back inside of the tent. I can't even look at his ass anymore."

Bren shot Aleric a nasty look and walked back with Xavier.

"I wish that I could say that I understand or sympathize with you Leric but I can't." said Chassidy.

Aleric was going to respond, but she turned around to walk away before he could get his words out.

"Baby I'll be standing right outside the tent watching if you need me, okay?" said Jeremy supportively.

"I'll be fine baby." Kara reassured

"Is she good Aleric?" asked Jeremy.

"Jeremy…you fractured my ribs, twisted my ankle and as you can see, gave me a black eye. There's not much I can do to anybody." said Aleric.

The two of them stared at each other for a few moments searching for the right words to say. She stood before him looking like a beautiful black angel, but for the life of him he couldn't utter a single word.

"I'm trying to think on where to start, Aleric. You…you have housed so much hate in your heart for the past three years that none of us even had a clue was there. You tried to ruin one of the most important relationships in my life. What kind of sick twisted person would pose as a friend, only to turn around and try to destroy our happiness? I would've expected something underhanded like this from Xavier, but not from you. No…not my Leric."

"Kara, I'm so…"

"I know what you're going to say and you should be. You should be sorry for all of this foolishness. You've hurt a lot of people, people who you will probably never have the chance to get back again."

"Kara I know, and I don't expect any of you to ever talk to me again. I just wanted you to know that I'm really sorry. I have some deeply rooted issues that I need to iron out. There are no excuses for what I've done."

"So you think it's that easy, huh? You think that you can act like a maniac for no freaking reason and then just bat those puppy dog eyes and apologize like it was nothing? Well if you think that then you have another thing coming. Just because you admit your craziness, it does not mean for one second that you're cleared of it...at least not with me."

"I know. I know everything that you're saying is the truth. I wish I had better reasons for what I did, but I don't. I just wanted to apologize to your face. I figured you deserved that much." said Aleric admittedly.

"Fair enough. Well I have to get back to the reception, my husband looks like he's about to go on a killing spree. Take care of yourself Aleric."

"You look good Kara."

"Thank you. Goodbye Aleric."

He watched her disappear into the tent with her husband. He was hurt but relieved. He wanted to be the one waking up to her every morning, yes, but he was glad he no longer had to hide his feelings. Aleric waited until his eyes lost her in the sea of people before walking away for good.

"Goodbye Kara, and congratulations on your new life."

EPILOGUE

"Is everyone sure they want to do this? We can all turn around, get back in our cars, and forget this entire thing." said Chassidy.

"You already know that I'm ready. Bren you ready?" asked Xavier.

"Do you really have to ask? Please! I'm good. Kara and Jeremy, are y'all ready?"

"Y'all act like we haven't been here before. Come on, let's go." said Jeremy.

Jeremy grabbed his wife's hand and left his friends arguing over who had more stamina and who was going to tap out first.

"Welcome back everybody. Ms. Eden is waiting for you all downstairs." said Cory.

They were familiar with The Pleasure Palace, so it took them no time to find the room Eden awaited them in.

"Chassidy hurry up and open the door. Hell from what you told us goes down in here, I'm ready to get started." said Bren.

PLEASURE PALACE

They walked inside of The Passion Pit and were immediately hit with high pitched moans and other sexual sound effects.

"Damn they are getting it in! Look at them over there by the bar."

Kara pointed towards a group of women gagged, tied up and being spanked by a masked individual. The masked stranger wore a strap on that she used to penetrate the mouths, pussies and anal holes of those bound women.

"Welcome once again my loves. How have you been?"

"Eden, miss us all with that bullshit. We know you had a hand in our dear friend Aleric's sick plan." said Kara.

"And I plan to make you pay for it for thirty days." said Xavier.

"Listen Kara and Jeremy, I'd just like to say..."

"Eden save it okay? We didn't come here to listen to you try to justify that bogus shit. You know why we're here, so just lead us to where we need to go." said Jeremy.

PLEASURE PALACE

"Chassidy knows where to go, don't you?" Eden revealed.

"Oh you're coming with us anyway, so you can lead the way." said Xavier.

Eden rolled her eyes and led them to a secluded room. When she opened the door everyone was greeted with a surprise. All of their pleasers were in this one room ready to rock their worlds.

"We were hoping we would see you again Chassidy. The fact that you look more relaxed than before just made my dick jump." said Kaleb.

"Kara I guess we aren't waiting until his birthday to have a threesome huh?" Elation asked elatedly.

"Oh my, Jeremy! Were you going to invite me to the birthday party?" asked Dior.

"Gotdamn! This is who y'all fucked the last time we were here? These chicks are bad!" said Xavier.

Bren's eyes locked with Savior's. He could sense her pussy was drooling. He mouthed the words, 'come get some' while making his dick jump. She pushed past Chassidy and walked towards him. Their lips touched before anything else. Deep off into an intense lip-lock, he scooped her into his arms and carried her to the bed.

"Well I guess those two don't need any ideas or games to kick off a fuck session. What about the rest of you?" asked Eden.

"Um, they got this. You just worry about what we're going to be doing." said Xavier.

"Anyway, there are toys, lubricants, food and wine to use on yourself and your pleaser. I'm horny and ready to get my socks knocked off so... you all are on your own." Eden said as she dropped her rob to the floor.

Xavier stood back and listened to Savior make Bren's kitten purr. He was jealous. He had always masked his attractions to her with arguments and jokes, but he couldn't deny it any longer. Tonight, she was his.
He placed his hand on Savior's shoulder.

"My turn."

Savior looked behind him with a hint of irritation in his eyes.

"Xavier what the hell are you doing?" Bren asked shocked.

"What? You're scared? Oh don't get scared now. You talked all of that shit about what you'd do to me and how I couldn't handle that pussy."

He pulled out his dick and straddled her.

"Now it's time to back up all of that shit talking and show and prove baby girl."

She nodded at his cock.

"Let me taste that."

"Be careful baby, because this dick right here causes extreme body convulsion, multiple orgasms, and creates stalkers. Make sure you're ready." said Xavier.

"Oh I'm ready. Are YOU ready because this pussy right here causes deep feelings and extreme happiness." she retorted.

"Quit talking shit and show me what that mouth do."

Without another word she pushed him backwards and took him in her mouth. She bobbed up and down on his tool with so much aggression that it sent chills throughout his entire body. He wrapped her hair around his hand guided her head up and down while thrusting his hips. She was better than he anticipated, so he had to take control and fast. Xavier yanked her up and onto her back. He was ready to consume her... ready to absorb every drop of her liquid love. He slurped her pussy like it was soup on a spoon. His tongue frantically wrote along her walls in cursive over and over. She'd shake and he'd scribe harder...faster...deeper.

"You want to moan. I see it in your face. Stop holding back. Sing to me baby."

Xavier sucked her until she arched her back and cursed. He came up for air and left a trail of kisses from her vagina to her lips. He lingered there, exploring her mouth as he slid on the condom. When he penetrated her she moaned his name against his lips.

"Say it again. Say my name."

"Xavier..." she whispered.

It was like a switch was flipped. He held her legs further apart and pushed in deeper.

"Mmm, shit, you're so deep. So...damn...deep."

He hid his face in the side of her neck and began to work her. They were so lost in each other that they didn't feel almost every pair of eyes in the room staring at them.

"What the hell? They aren't fucking, they are making love." said Eden.

"Jealous are we?' Savior said teasingly.

"No, but you obviously are. You haven't taken your eyes off them yet." Eden shot back.

Kara couldn't believe that she was watching two of her best friends have sex. She couldn't help but to be turned on by the intensity and passion they exuded. Touching herself, her mouth and her pussy watered. Her breath caught in her throat when Jeremy pressed his manhood against her ass. He bit her neck and squeezed her vagina. The feel of him always made her light headed. Knowing that, he caught her just in time when her knees gave way. The two of them laid on the floor right where they were and went crazy. They kissed and groped each other like two horny high school kids.

"Can we join in?" asked Elation.

Dior knelt next to Jeremy and kissed him...then Kara...then Elation. Those lip-locks set them all ablaze. The beast within them all had been unleashed and shit was getting animalistic.

Chassidy was led by Kaleb to the other side of the room. Xaria, Blake, Jock, Cameron and Amarie were all waiting with the 'I'm ready to fuck the shit out you...AGAIN' look on their faces. They immediately swarmed Chassidy like vultures to a dead carcass kissing, licking, and biting every inch of her being. Amarie poured honey on the top half of her, chocolate on her mid-section and sprayed whip cream on her lower half. They feasted on her like they were prisoners having their last meal. Their tongues and fingers played tag inside of her pussy, driving her up the wall.

Eden pointed out Savior's jealousy, but her own was starting to show on her face. Ever since that night a few weeks ago she craved Xavier. No man had ever controlled and ruled over her in the sex department, he did both so effortlessly that she wanted more. She pulled Xavier's mouth from Bren's and tongued him down. Kissing him slowed down his rhythm until she eventually got him to stop. He pulled out of Bren and pushed Eden's head between her legs.

"Eat her." he demanded.

Eden followed orders and melted into Bren. With her swollen clit already extremely sensitive, Bren grabbed a handful of Eden's hair and pushed her face deeper into her. Xavier licked Eden's asshole and pussy until it was dripping with her juices and his saliva. He popped her ass cheeks with his dick head before inserting it into her pussy and his middle finger into her asshole.

"Shit! Right there! Oooh shit your tongue is strong." shouted Bren.

Eden was relieved when Bren finally came, because she was coming up on her own nut and she wanted to enjoy it. Once again Xavier made unfamiliar sounds bolt from her mouth while he drove her body to severe vibration.

"Yea, I told you I was going to beat this shit up! Your pussy loves this dick. It will come for it every time." said Xavier.

Eden transferred her screams to Bren when their mouths connected. Bren found Eden's clit and attacked it.

"Aaahhhhh shiiittttt!!!!" Eden screamed and squirted massively.

Xavier backed out of Eden and took the condom off. He held his nut for Bren. He was on a mission to finally bust inside of her like he'd fantasized on many nights. He lay on top of Bren and showered her with kisses. Rolling over, he pulled her on top of him and feasted on her hardened breasts.

"I made you say my name, now make me say yours. Ride me baby...ride me until I can't take it anymore."
His words made her pussy throb. She'd gotten back hot, wet, and horny and she was ready to give him what he asked for.

Amarie sat on Chassidy's face and Cameron penetrated her at the same time. Amarie was telling Chassidy how good her tongue felt when her voice became muffled. Blake had placed himself in her mouth.

PLEASURE PALACE

Xaria was howling from having two monstrous cocks inside of her at once. Jock was wrecking her from the front and Kaleb worked her out from the back.

"Chassidy, whatever you're doing, keep doing it. She's sucking the shit out of my dick...." Blake said hoarsely.

Chassidy couldn't respond even if she tried. Cameron was banging her g-spot like she owed him an orgasm, and Amarie's entire weight rested on her face, and it was hard for her to breathe.

Amarie took Blake's dick out of her mouth and stroked him hard and fast with two hands. The closer she came to her peak, the quicker her hands moved up and down his shaft. All of a sudden she screamed and Chassidy's mouth was filled with warm gooeyness.

Blake and Cameron were both moaning in unison. Blake forced Amarie's mouth onto him and oozed his hot seed down her throat, thrusting none-stop until he fell against the wall in exhaustion.

"Come on Cameron...cum with me baby...cum with me."

PLEASURE PALACE

He went into speed racer mode and pushed them both over ecstasy's edge.

"Oh my God Cameron!" she yelled.

He huskily repeated her name in her ear again and again, until he could no longer move or speak.

They all turned their attention when Xaria let out a high pitched scream. Her cum poured out like a waterfall. Kaleb held her against his chest tightly as he sprayed inside of her and Jock yelled out obscenities before falling to his knees.

"Damn, good job boys." said Chassidy.

Kara was riding Jeremy backwards while she ate out Dior. Jeremy had his hands full thrusting his dick into his wife and his tongue into Elation. Elation rocked back and forth on Jeremy's face like she was doing the Tootsie Roll. The way they were both working him drew out the animal in him. He took turns smacking both their asses while turning up his tongue and dick game. All of the ladies' moans were in sync like a choir.

PLEASURE PALACE

Elation leaned forward and popped her ass on his lips until she trembled violently from satisfaction.

When Elation freed up his face, he sat up and wrapped his hands around Dior's ass, smashing her crotch deeper into Kara's face. He pumped into his wife with so much force that she'd stop eating Dior just to let out a scream or two. Dior's knees were wobbly and her hands were gripping Kara's hair tighter as she edged closer to a climax.

"Oooh weeeee...I'm about to cum...Kara don't stop...don't you fucking stop!"

Dior threw her head back and began to look like she was throwing a tempera-tantrum. Her body jerked until she fell to the floor from the momentum. She gathered enough strength to crawl over to Elation and tongue kisses her. Elation held Dior as they watched Kara and Jeremy rage into earth shattering orgasms.

"Fuck Kara... I love you... I love you so much."

"I love you too baby...take it...take this nut...it's yours."

PLEASURE PALACE

She closed her eyes tightly and enjoyed the ride. He went in and out of her like he had a point to prove, and he did. He let her know that it was his pussy forever. Kara leaned back, locked her wrist around her husband's neck and fell apart. Their orgasms were so strong that anyone would've thought they were being electrocuted. They shivered and quivered against each other until their bodies went limp. They rested quietly, stroking each other's faces and wearing crooked smiles.

Jeremy and Kara sat up and watched the show with everyone else. Bren and Xavier were making mad passionate love and it captured everyone's attention. He had Bren hitting some serious high notes, but everyone was so consumed in their own ecstasy that they didn't pay attention to the others having sex.

Bren rode him like a professional. He said her name back to back to back and throbbed so hard that she felt it deep within her. They were now rolling around from one end of the bed to the next snatching sounds of pleasure out of each other with every kiss and nibble. Xavier finally penned her down and merged into her with aggression.

"You're mine. I'm not sharing! I'm stingy. I'm so...fucking...stingy. Oh God Xavier..." she said against his lips.

"I'm all yours baby, I promise. Now give me what I need. Give me what belongs to me. I need it baby...so bad."

He kissed angrily.

"I love you Bren. Don't you cum until you tell me that you love me too; you better say it dammit!"

"I love you Xavier! I love you! I love you! I love you!"

He let out a growl and released himself into her moist center. She followed suit and creamed all over his manhood. They exchanged many more soft I love you's before lying silently in a warm embrace.

Eden saw the disappointed look on Savior's face and approached him.

"Often we want things that we never had a chance of ever getting in the first place."

She grabbed him by the hand and placed it on her hard nipples.

"How about we leave these two love birds alone and go up to my office and fuck until we pass out."

"Sounds like a good idea."

Savior took one last look at Bren and left.

"I'm glad you two finally came to your senses! Now we all don't have to be subjected to you two fighting like cats and dogs every zero point five seconds!" yelled Chassidy.

"Amen to that sister." Jeremy agreed.

"This has been on my Sunday morning prayer list for years now." Kara admitted.

Everyone erupted into laughter.

"Gosh, were they that bad?" asked Xaria.

"Chile you have no idea. Some days we thought we'd have to bail one of them out of jail for killing the other." said Chassidy.

"Okay I really need for you all to stop talking about us like we're not here." said Bren.

"That's okay baby let them talk. They are just hating because we showed them how to make REAL love." said Xavier.

Bren snuggled up to Xavier and smacked him on the ass.

"So what's next for us? You love me and I love you. Are we going to prove it or not? Well… I did prove that I loved you a lot by that huge nut I pulled up out of you." said Bren.

"I'm willing to prove it, and if you're willing to join in and prove that you really want me...really want us, then you never know, Kara might not be the only married woman in the crew. And for your information, I made you bust the biggest nut. Matter of fact, the longest nut you've ever busted...EVER!" he responded.

"Oh really?! Well let's go at it again and see who the beast is and who the prey is. I'm more than willing to prove it. I've wanted this to happen between us for a long time, but I was just too damn stubborn to admit it. I'm really glad that this happened, Xavier."

PLEASURE PALACE

"I am too Bren. I wouldn't take back tonight for anything in the world. I also wouldn't challenge me like you just did."

Their kisses went from gentle to hungry and they were beginning to light that sexual fire between them again.

"Um you guys, let's leave these new love birds alone and start some trouble in the other rooms." Chassidy suggested.

Chassidy, Kara and Jeremy were the last ones to leave out of Orgy Central.

"Aye kids, neither one of us are ready to be an auntie or an uncle, so wrap it up will ya?!" Kara shouted.

Both Bren and Xavier gave Kara the finger without breaking their intense lip-lock.

"Yep! We love y'all too! Bye!" Kara said shutting the door behind her.

The rest of the night until closing Jeremy, Kara and Chassidy, drank, ate and made love to strangers. They decided before leaving that what happened inside of Pleasure Palace stayed inside of Pleasure Palace. If anything got out to their other friends and family they would deny it. After all, they'd managed to keep the freaks in them on the low for this long. Everyone was happy and high off of sex. Desires were met and fulfilled, lovers grew closer together, and new loves began. The three of them left the club that morning without Bren and Xavier. Apparently they weren't done proving who loved each other the most.

CHAT IT UP!
~Book club discussion questions~

I.   **Did you enjoy Pleasure Palace? Why or why not?**

II.   **Is Obsession's writing style easy to get into? Is it familiar or different from your usual read?**

III.   **Would you want to meet any of the characters? Did you like or hate them?**

IV.   **Which passage of Pleasure Palace stood out the most? How did it help you decide if you liked or disliked the book?**

V.   **Are there any situations, characters, or experiences in the book that you can relate to? If yes, how?**

VI.   **Did you learn anything knew?!**

VII.   **Did the story bring out any emotions within you?**

VIII.   **Why do you think Obsession chose Pleasure Palace as the title? Would you title it differently?**

IX.   **Did the book end the way you expected? Would you have preferred an alternate ending?**

X.   **Would you recommend Pleasure Palace to other readers, family, friends, neighbors or co-workers?**

XI.   **If you could ask Obsession one question, what would it be?**

XII.   **What word would you use to describe Pleasure Palace?**

<u>WORKS IN PROGRESS...</u>

<u>THE ~PLEASE ME~ SHORT STORY SERIES</u>

*THEY CALL IT KING (The book of ALERIC)

*INSATIABLE BEAST (The book of EDEN)

*11 ½ INCHES (The book of SAVIOR)

*JAW DROPPER (The book of ELATION)

*IN MOURNING: The sex, love & pain of Obsession
(This poetry book will bring you deeper into me more so than the ones before)

**AVAILABLE ON AMAZON
IN KINDLE & PAPERBACK**

If you were given only six months to a year to live, what would be your final good deed?

Filled with love, humor and heart stopping suspense, you will find Gail Washington; a therapist diagnosed with a

monstrous disease. She arranges a sensual mixer in hopes that four individuals, who are also her clients, make a love connection. Nathaniel, a head strong seductive pediatric surgeon, has never met a woman that could handle him mentally or physically; that's why Gail's feisty secretary Zaya is perfect for him. Raven is the top male tennis player in the world. He quickly learns that with championships comes a lot of money and a lot of women; both of which he's always had control over until he meets Morgan, a free spirited hairstylist that is drop dead gorgeous and emotionally elusive.

Will Gail live to see her last wish granted? Will they surrender their hearts and fall passionately in love with one another? Or will Gail's final act of kindness accompany her to the grave?"

EXCERPT:

PLEASURE PALACE

Upon entering their home, she hears a familiar song playing softly in their bedroom.

"Aw, he must have heard my voicemail and decided to play our favorite song. He knows Janet Jackson always cheers me up."

She sings along with the lyrics as she climbs the stairs to their bedroom.

"Anytime, and any place, I don't care who's around…"

She stops singing when she hears moaning on the other side of the door.

Turning the door knob slowly, she stands outside of the room in complete and utter shock; her husband is getting head from someone submerged under their bed covers. Quietly closing the door, she heads downstairs to her office.

"This bastard just can't stop cheating can he?" she mutters while opening the safe hidden under her desk. She retrieves the .22 her father gave her before she was married for protection, because she lived alone. Loaded and ready, all she had to do was take the safety off and shoot.

Gail crept slowly back up to the bedroom; she stands outside of the door re-thinking her actions. Just as she decides that it isn't worth going to jail for she hears, "Oooooo Monroe, you're about to make me cum." Covering her mouth, she speaks through the spaces between her fingers.

"Monroe? It can't be."

Enraged she burst into the bedroom and points the gun at her husband.

"Gail! Oh my gosh! What are you doing here?! Baby it's not what it looks like."

"Bastard I live here, that's what I'm doing here and it's EXACTLY what it looks like." Her aim switches from her husband to the covers.

"Monroe come from under the covers and reveal your backstabbing, trifling face. My own brother caught giving fallacio to my husband...how could you?"

Emerging from under the covers with a sinister smile, Monroe lays his head on Chaz's chest.

"Well how couldn't I? He is just too sexy! Gail I'm sorry, but I had to give him a real orgasm because from what he tells me, he's been faking it for a long time now. Plus I grew tired of wondering how he tasted… so here we are."

Monroe flips the covers to the side disclosing him and Chaz nakedness. He walks over to the dresser and pauses the iPod playing before slipping on his t-shirt and shorts; sitting on the edge of bed he puts on his shoes and gazes up at his sister.

"Gail, Chile, put that gun away. All three of us know that you won't hurt a fly, and besides, how would it look if the beautiful thirty seven year old Gail Washington, owner and founder of "The Healing Center," a member of the Distinguished American Psychological Association, an avid volunteer in her community and the best damn psychologist in all of Chicago land, shoot her homosexual younger brother for sleeping with her cheating no good husband? Darling all that you've worked for will be shot to hell. Your life will be ruined, so put the gun away and get a divorce. " he says.

She slowly lowers the gun as he pushes past her to exit the room. Half way down the stairs Monroe looks back at his lover and sister to further taunt her.

"Oh and Honey, he taste delicious!"

Unhooked: A twisted love story (formerly titled prostitutes anonymous. It is in the process of getting a new cover)

A self-employed young hooker working the streets of Chicago, Lydia adapts to the grimy life of prostitution easily and has no intention of walking away from the profession. That is, until one of her high paying johns Max confesses that he's madly in love with her and can offer her things that she's only dreamed of; like FREE unconditional love. When she falls victim to her lifestyle but refuses to give it up, Max takes matters into his own hands and blackmails her into choosing to turn her life around instead choosing to turn tricks. In this romantic comedy, author

PLEASURE PALACE

Obsession delivers a humorous story of a young girls quest to discover if loving herself and somebody else is worth retiring her hooker heels.

Excerpt:
"Whoever said that you can't turn a hoe into a house wife didn't choose the right hoe to try with. Whoever said you can't turn a trick into a treat is a hater because he obviously tried and failed, you see her right there?"
Says Pastor Passion.
Lydia looks to her right to see a light skin woman with shoulder length blonde dreadlocks smiling at the pastor.

"That's Miranda; I use to call her my bottom hoe but now I call her my wife. She's living proof that with love, patience and prayer, you can unhook a hooker and turn her into an honest woman. Stand up honey and introduce yourself, but first shake it for them a little bit."
Lydia watches Pastor Passion's eyes light up at the sight of his wife making it clap. She gives Max a nudge in the side when she notices him cracking up.

"You see, she use to get X-rated for any Tom, Tammy, Dick, Harry and Henrietta but now she only gets nasty for me. Go ahead baby, tell them a little about yourself." Pastor Passion switches places with his wife and flicks his tongue out making her shiver.

"Oh God, I think I'm going to be sick." Lydia says.

Max taps her on the knee while laughing, "Oh this is just the beginning, there's more!"

"Hi everyone my name is Miranda, and I'm a recovered prostitute for ten years and counting. My husband had me working hard on my knees for twenty years. It didn't matter man or woman, for fifteen minutes and three hundred dollars, I did whatever you wanted me to. For a young girl who didn't love herself and had no self-esteem; earning a few Benjamin's in less than thirty minutes made me feel somewhat validated. Now I adore myself and I happily slob my husband's knob for free!"

"And she's good at it too y'all. Thank you baby, you can have a seat; will anyone else like to share their story? How about you young lady with the red yeast infection shorts on with the stomach that's looking like an angry prune; why don't you say a few words." Says Pastor Passion. Lydia looks over at Max and he has tears in his eyes from laughing so hard. The chick that Pastor Passion put on blast makes Lydia's stomach do somersaults when she walks past. The smell of fish and must rushed inside of her nose making her dizzy and queasy. Apparently everyone else in the room gets a whiff of her funk because every face was scowling or being covered up.

"STOP RIGHT WHERE YOU ARE!" Yells Pastor Passion, "You must have busted it wide open before you came to this meeting. Matter of fact, a few of you all did, I can smell the juices all the way up here. There are some boxes of Summer Eve's in the first bathroom in the back; use them!" Lydia's mouth drops wide open when half the room stands up.

"This don't make no damn sense! It's only five boxes back there so y'all are gonna have to puff puff pass!" Says Pastor Passion. By this time Max is doubled over in his chair rolling, he hasn't noticed the horrid look on Lydia's face. Pastor continues to ramble on about how he use to do a smell check on all of his hoes daily. The fresher the clit, the more money that's spent. He waits for all of the ladies to file back in before addressing the room.

"Before ending this meeting I would like to say to the newbies that here at S.T.T.I, we require the participation and completion of our twelve step program called, Unhooking Hookers. This program will work to free you from your addiction to instant love, money and not the pussy popping lifestyle. For whatever reason or reasons you became a hooker will no long matter once you've graduated. I look forward to teaching you all how to quit being a heaux. And remember, when your pimp starts singing "I'd rather pimp you oohhh yeaaahh, said I'd rather pimp with youuuuuuu" just walk away! Good day everybody, I'm out!"

6 degrees of separation...

Satisfyingly explicit, this bon-a-fide narrative is plagued with humor, sex, romance, violence, devastating family secrets and more. Inspirational in its own right, this urban tale will invite readers into the lives of six individuals, who learn from one another; that with love, faith, and forgiveness...peace found within will outweigh all the pain that was ever endured.

EXCERPT:

Ethan stood behind Thailand to hear his conversation. Thailand was expressing to another couple why the painting they were interested in purchasing was one of his favorites.

"I think this is a good choice. It can go in any room of the house, with the exception of the kitchen." Thailand continued. "And don't worry, I'm not spitting game. I'm not into fucking up other people's money." Ethan stopped in mid sip of his champagne. Those words echoed in his mind, 'fucking up other people's money'.

"Brooklyn, hold this glass." Ethan tapped Thailand on the shoulder.

"What's up man, you thinking of finishing the job?" Ethan asked. Thailand frowned.

"Excuse me. Do I know you?"

"Yea you know me homie. You tried to kill me when we were kids, remember?" Thailand's glass shattered on the floor.

"E...Ethan?"

"Yea it's me." Brooklyn could see that Ethan was furious because he had the same look in his eyes in the boxing ring. She pushed her way through the crowd and found Aaron and Derricka.

"Aaron, Ethan is about to hurt Thailand! Apparently Thai tried to murder Ethan years ago." Brooklyn said frantically.

"What?! What the fuck?! Where are they?!" Brooklyn guided Aaron to where they were, then they saw a broken window, and Ethan on top of Thailand.

"Man I told you that night that I was forced to do it! Because if I didn't, they were

going to kill me! I'm sorry man! I'm sorry!"
Thailand said pleadingly.

"I should kill you! I should fucking
kill you!" "Ethan baby please, look at me.
Can we talk about this?"

"Fuck that Brooklyn." Ethan yelled.

"What the fuck is going on?!"
Adriana asked. Ethan kicked Thailand in the
stomach.

"Answer her!"

"Fourteen years ago, I tried to kill
Ethan. My mother was a drug addict and she
was in debt with some big time drug dealers.
In order for her debt to be wiped clean, I had
to knock off their rival drug dealer, who was
Ethan. If I didn't kill him, they were going to
kill me and my mother, but I fled the state
that night, so they didn't catch me." Thailand
explained. Everyone in the studio stood
silently in shock.

"Now that's a man. You should've
been in the army son. What's your name?
Ethan? We could've used a cold mutha like
you." Aaron spun around.

"Dad? What are you doing here, and who is that?" Brooklyn couldn't believe her eyes, it was Lana.

"Lana what are you doing with Aaron's father? And he's married!" said Brooklyn.

"Anthony, you told me you were divorced and didn't have any children." said Lana.

"Yea, that's the same thing he told me. That's why we are no longer together." Everyone looked at Adriana. Thailand stood up.

"This is the older man you were in a relationship with for three years?"

"Three years?! Three muthafuck...You bastard! You've always treated my mother like shit!" screamed Aaron.

"Yes! And I will continue to do so. I pull the strings on your mother. Always have and always will." Aaron lunged at Anthony, but was restrained by Ethan.

"Anthony, get your trifling ass up out if here! Get out my got damn studio! Everybody get out! Get the fuck out!"

Brooklyn walked up to Anthony and smacked the shit out of him. Everybody stared at her.

"What?! What the he'll y'all looking at? Somebody needed to smack his stupid ass."

If you thought that you knew Brooklyn, Ethan, Aaron, Derricka, Thailand and Adriana… well think again. In this highly anticipated sequel to Climatic Successions, you will discover that love not only changes but exposes individuals for who they truly are. Greed… temptation… insecurities… lies and

unresolved issues have created a maze that if the wrong path is chosen, it can lead to catastrophic consequences. Will they find treasures within trials and tribulations? Or will their love fail and all they've worked and wished for be in vain?

EXCERPT:

Adriana hadn't slept in days. Thailand hadn't returned any of her texts or phone calls, and Aaron's status hadn't changed. Since the day she could hold a paintbrush, Adriana had painted her pain until she couldn't muscle up the strength to stroke any longer. She put her hair in a ponytail and pulled a stool up to a blank canvas. A heart shattered into pieces is what she felt and so she would paint. Short or long, every brush stroke helped her breathe a little easier. A knock at the door startled her, causing her to drop the paint brush onto her pants.

"Shit. WHO IS IT?!" she yelled.

"Hello, I'm looking for Ms. Adriana Jackson?" the voice on the other end said.

"I'm sorry, but the gallery isn't open today, Tuesday through Saturday only." Adriana stated, annoyed by the interruption.

"Oh I know. I was hoping to talk to her about creating a painting for a special friend of mine; Aaron." Well shit, now I have to open the door, thought Adriana.

"Hi, I'm Adriana."

"Yes, I know. I've always wanted to meet you. Your work is well known all over Chicago. It is an honor."

"Thank you. Please come in."
You're going to regret this. Once I'm done with you, no one will be able to recognize you, the visitor thought.

"So how do you know Aaron?" Adriana wanted to know.

"I'm a regular at his restaurant. The menu and entertainment are exquisite, can't get enough of the place."

"Yea his place is one of the best in all of downtown Chicago. I take it you two are pretty cool?"

"Oh yea, we share a passion for art. He never shut up about his all-time favorite painter, Ms. Adriana Jackson. After hearing about his tragic accident, couple of the other regulars and I thought it would be nice to chip in and ask you to create an exclusive piece to hang inside his restaurant."

"That is so sweet. Of course I will create a piece on you guys' behalf. It will be free of charge."

"Oh no! You don't have to do that. We are more than willing to pay you for your services, Ms. Jackson."

"No, no I insist. What concept did you all come up with?"

"Well we all thought that whatever you came up with would be fitting. Your work is known for exuding strength through pain, triumphs over tribulations, persevering through the storm; you know things of that nature. I think you should paint like it's your very last time. It just might be."

"What do you mean by...?" Pain rushed through Adriana's head like a freight train. Dizzy with blood dripping in her eyes, she tried to get up off the floor.

"Who...who are you?"

"Who am I? When you opened that door, I became the worst decision you've

ever made, that's who I am!" She struck
Adriana again, causing her to black out.
Standing over her, she began to go off into a
rant.

I~AM~OBSESSION

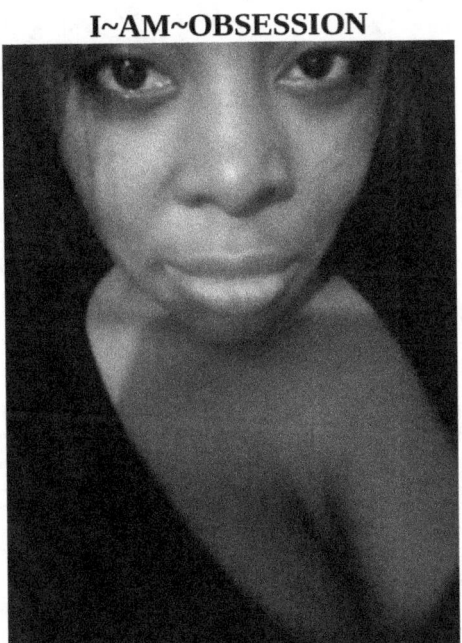